BONDS

CRAVE

FOUR POWERFUL AND DOMINATING BILLIONAIRES
ONE UNBREAKABLE BOND

SIERRA
CARTWRIGHT

USA TODAY BESTSELLING AUTHOR

CRAVE

DEDICATION

For the friendships I've made along the way.

PROLOGUE

"That's the most ridiculous thing I've ever heard you say. Spectacular in its stupidity. Borderline insane, even. You've had some idiotic moments in the last four years, but even for you, this is remarkable." He waved a hand. "What in the *hell* are you thinking?"

Sarah hadn't expected her old friend Julien to be wildly enthusiastic about her request to hook her up with her former boyfriend, but this? "Don't hold back," she returned, reaching for the bottle of wine. Like everything in Julien Bonds' life, the Merlot, a brand she'd never heard of and couldn't pronounce, was expensive.

"Sweetling, I haven't even yet begun," he said as she poured wine into her glass.

"Sweetling?"

"Better than piranha, I should think."

"Piranha?" she asked, stung. "Is that how you see me?"

"Well, you don't really have the teeth for it, do you? So I settled for sweetling."

"That doesn't fit me, either."

"You're right. I'm back to the man-eating carnivore image, then."

"Sweetling it is," she agreed.

He grinned. He'd won this skirmish, but she intended to win the bigger battle.

Glass in hand, she sat back and curled her bare legs beneath her. The white leather couch was smooth, soft, more inviting than her host. Well, that wasn't exactly true. He *had* agreed to see her, even though she'd had to accommodate his bizarre schedule and leave a party she'd been attending in northern California.

When she'd exited his private elevator, the bottle had already been uncorked and waiting. So he wasn't completely inhospitable.

Julien pressed his palms together and regarded her across his fingertips. Although it was in the ever-expanding heart of Silicon Valley, his sprawling office suite at 1, Bonds Street was every bit as eclectic as he was. The building itself was only a year old. Rather than opting for a traditional structure, Julien had instructed his team of architects to design something that looked more like a UFO than a corporate headquarters.

This portion of Julien's space was streamlined, decorated in white, chrome and glass. A shocking blood-red rug that cost at least as much as her yearly mortgage payment was splashed across the white marble floor.

Here he had no clutter, not even a magazine.

His desk was about half of a football field away. Its vast surface was covered with electronics that looked as if they were in various stages of development.

A silk-screened Chinese partition blocked off the back of the room. Behind its expanse, she knew, was a creative and frightening workspace. She'd seen it once and had been taken aback by the disaster. Papers had been scattered on every flat surface, tossed on the floor, tacked to the walls, taped to the tables, wadded and tossed in the general direction of an overflowing garbage can.

A mattress, sheathed with twelve hundred thread-count sheets, lay shoved against a wall. He kept it on hand for the times—days—that he was so involved in a project that he didn't go home.

It was a good thing his office had a shower and a closet full of suits as well as sweatpants. He could greet the President of the United States or do a presentation to the city council then go back to his slovenly and strange ways, including eating celery and peanut butter for two meals a day.

Still, he was the best sort of friend, and he had been since she'd first met him four years before. He'd had an appointment with her boss, Reece McRae, and he'd apologized for showing up early. She'd stood there, files clutched against her chest, speechless, trapped somewhere between star-struck and awestruck. But Julien had helped himself to a glass of Scotch and had told her tales of his college days with Reece.

In the hour it had taken Reece to arrive, Julien had charmed her and extracted all her secrets. Rather than turn up his nose at her financial struggle to put herself through college, he'd told her he admired her scrappy determination. She'd walked away from the meeting believing none of the nasty things said about him in the press, though he assured her that he really was an evil bastard who chewed the heads off his competitors.

Now, four years later, he'd be the first person she'd call if she needed bail money. She knew he'd insist on hearing all the gritty, salacious details before he sprang her loose. But he'd be there.

"I have to point out that there are more than seven billion people on the planet," he continued, still regarding her. "I should think at least half of them are men. Even if you discount those who are outside your age range, married or gay, I'd say you could have your choice of, at least five hundred million eligible bachelors."

"True."

"And you want one in specific."

"Yes." She took a drink of her wine. *Reece.*

"There has to be a line of men a dozen deep who want to take you out."

"I don't want to go on dates." She sighed in exasperation. "Are you listening at all?"

"Why didn't you say so? You want to be fucked. Surely there's someone out there who would be willing to do that. Someone. Anyone." He reached for his phone, a slim, super-secret model the press would kill to get its hands on. Rumors of the device's existence had swirled in cyberspace for two months. Last week an enterprising tech writer had broken into one of the building's clean rooms to steal a prototype. The intruder had walked away from the evening with a police record and photos of a replicated communication device from a 1970s science fiction movie. Julien had told the story with unabashed glee, somewhere around, oh, six hundred times. "You're"—he glanced at her—"considered passably attractive at least. Aren't you?"

"Julien!"

"Right. You're not bad at all." He thumbed through several screens. "Wait. Wait. I'm sure I can find someone to dip his wick in your honeypot."

She rolled her eyes. She would have laughed, but that would only encourage him. "Don't quit your day job."

"No chance," he responded without looking up. "Let's see. Ah. Got it." He lowered his phone and smiled.

Absently she wondered how many thousands of dollars

had gone into his veneers. She'd heard that he'd had several teeth knocked out during his younger days.

"Sylvio Aiello."

"He has a little dick."

He lowered his head and pantomimed looking over the rim of a pair of glasses. "A little dick?"

She held her thumb and forefinger about two inches part.

"That small?"

"Maybe a bit bigger. Not much."

"You slept with Sylvio?"

Sarah shuddered. "Oh hell no. But Melissa did." She and Mel had shared an apartment while they'd attended college, and they still worked together on projects.

"Mel?"

"Yep."

"Your friend? Business partner? That Mel?"

"Yes."

"Christ. I thought she had better taste than that."

"Wait. Did you just tell me I should sleep with him?"

"Yes. But not Mel. I thought she had better taste than you do. Besides, I thought she fancied me."

Sarah nodded. "She does like men with two commas in their net worth." She smiled. "Regardless of the size of their dick."

"Are you insinuating…?"

"Not at all. I'm just saying that money trumps anatomy."

Julien opened his mouth but then shut it again before nodding and saying, "Right. We'll remove Sylvio from consideration."

"He was never in consideration."

"There has to be someone who'll fuck you."

She threw a pillow at him.

Ignoring her, he scrolled some more. "Oh. Right. Right, right, right. I've got it. Sanders."

She choked on a sip of her wine. "No. Not now. Not ever."

"It's the twitch, isn't it?"

"Ah…" Words failed her. She wanted to be nice. She'd met Bart Sanders twice. He'd seemed a decent sort.

"Unfortunate, that."

"Yes." It was. As Bart became more excited, at the poker table or with a woman, his left eye twitched. If you watched, it got worse, until his whole body shook. "I got vertigo the one time I went dancing with him. He moved in for a kiss and—"

"Right." He swiped the screen again. "Marvin Zeitgeist."

"That's not even his real name. What kind of architect uses a pseudonym?"

"A successful one." He quirked an eyebrow.

"Just stop," she begged, taking another sip. "I want Reece."

Julien slid his phone onto the table. "So our Reece has no twitch, uses his real name and presumably has a big dick."

"No comment."

"I think I need some of that wine now." He reached for the bottle and topped off his glass. Then, staring at her with an intensity that made her shiver, his tone much more serious, he asked, "What makes you think I'll help you destroy my friend again?"

Destroy? That's what had happened to her hopes and dreams. Before answering, she took a steadying breath. "That's a bit extreme, isn't it?"

"Is it?" he countered.

Over the last few months, she'd been following Reece's companies and his career on social media. The man was doing ridiculously well for himself. He had stocks that had recently doubled in value.

"You weren't here," Julien said bluntly. "You left without a word, and the rest of us had to pick up the pieces. For a long time, you didn't even answer my calls. I had to hire a private investigator to make sure your dead body wasn't in a ravine somewhere."

"It was about self-preservation."

"Pardon me if I call it balls-to-the-wall rude."

"You're right." She winced. "I was thinking only of myself and making sure Reece didn't find me."

He shrugged. "I'm not sure I've completely forgiven you, to be honest."

His forthright admission didn't surprise her. Julien was world-renowned for his many talents, but tact was not among them. Sarah countered with, "You've never asked why I ran."

Julien poured himself a glass of wine then and leaned back. Despite the fact that it was midnight, he looked fresh in his crisp white shirt, black wool pants, and polished-to-a-gloss, likely by him, leather wingtips. His top two buttons were undone, and if he'd had on a tie at any point, there was no sign of it. At least tonight he wasn't wearing one of his T-shirts with the sleeves cut off.

"Five minutes," he invited. "Enlighten me. Convince me that I should have anything to do with your insanity. Otherwise you never mention it again."

Realizing she might never get another chance, she looked into her glass then back at him before admitting, "He wanted more than I could give."

"Go on."

"He had certain tastes…" She didn't know how much Julien knew about Reece's Dominant nature and what he demanded from his women. Hell, even she'd struggled to understand. She still did, if she was honest with herself. Finally, she settled for, "Expectations. They went beyond the traditional marriage roles."

"All relationships have a unique dynamic. Adults talk about them. Negotiate."

"Not everything can be negotiated."

"It can," he countered.

He'd become a gazillionaire off that philosophy. "You've never had absolutes? Rules?" she asked.

"Go on."

"Things you wouldn't tolerate, no matter what?"

Julien narrowed his eyes. "Did he physically harm you?"

"Good God, no." Not in the way Julien meant.

"So the reason you couldn't give him the courtesy of an in-person breakup is…?" He trailed off. "Even a text message would have been less heartless."

Heavy and thick, the silence shrouded her. Julien didn't speak, and she had a sense that he wouldn't.

"I panicked. I wasn't thinking past the urge for self-preservation." She stared into the depths of her wine. "If I'd have tried to talk to him, he would have stopped me."

"It's been, what, a couple of years?" Julien asked.

Two years, three months, ten days.

"Why now?" he asked.

His relaxed demeanor didn't fool her. This was a man whose interest was always keen. He missed nothing.

"Business. I need an infusion of cash."

"Ask me. I may have some spare change lying around."

"This fits with Reece's portfolio better than yours."

"And what about your need for self-preservation? Money trumps all?"

Sarah exhaled. "Fine. You're right. It's not about the money. That was an excuse."

"And a bad one at that. I'm waiting."

"I'm smarter now." She worried her upper lip. "More grown up. More capable of admitting to myself what I need and want."

"That demands honesty."

"It does."

8

"So try some with me."

Sarah should have known that Julien would never go for a shallow answer. Despite the fact that the media painted him as a hedonist, the man was complex. She exhaled then leaned forward to slide the glass onto the table. "I've not met anyone his equal."

"I can believe that."

"I miss him." The emotional connection, the physical intimacy, the brilliance of their brainstorming sessions.

Julien shrugged at that. "That's a logical consequence of your choice."

"I understand your need to protect him." Exasperation tied her patience into a knot. But losing her temper with Julien wouldn't help her get any closer to Reece. "I wish I'd been stronger back then. But it took being away from him to evolve into the person I am now. I tried everything I could think of to reach him. Phone. Internet. Email." Reece's silence had made her realize that the intervening years hadn't softened his attitude toward her. The man was measured and calculating in everything he did. On the rare occasions that she'd angered him, he'd shown his displeasure by keeping distance between them. She'd seen him freeze out associates, friends, even a distant family member in the same way. After one argument, she'd called him Iceman, a title he hadn't disagreed with. "I was even desperate enough to stop by the house we used to share," she confessed.

"He moved."

"I discovered that for myself." She grimaced at the memory. It had taken weeks to convince herself that she should try to see him when she'd taken a business trip to Houston.

Since she'd had an extra hour to spare before her flight home, she'd driven to the house they'd shared. She'd been stunned when the new owner had told her he'd lived there for over a year.

Graciously, the man had invited her in. Given that he was a stranger, older than her father by at least a decade and had been scratching his belly with one hand and holding a can of beer in the other while his shorts hung off his visible hip bones, she'd refused. As if that wasn't bad enough, the bird of paradise she'd planted when she had lived there had died from obvious neglect.

Julien waited.

"Look, I made a mistake. A big one. And I'm ready to admit it," she said.

There was more. She'd recently been talking to one of her clients, Loretta. The woman was in her sixties, and she'd passed up the opportunity to marry a gentleman friend ten years previously. Loretta had refused his proposal and had asked him to wait. She'd told him she'd finally managed to get her children grown and gone, and now it was time for her to follow the dream of starting her own business.

Loretta had confessed she'd just spent her birthday alone. She'd called her former boyfriend, only to learn that he hadn't waited. He was happily married, and he'd added that he and his wife had bought motorcycles and planned to tour the United States. Loretta had warned Sarah that life went by too quickly. Ten years had vanished without her realizing it.

The conversation had left a terrible, gnawing sensation in the pit of her stomach that grew worse every day. She knew she wouldn't be satisfied until she'd reached out to Reece.

"Look, Julien, I'm sure you've never screwed up then wanted to make amends later."

"Actually, no. Not that I can remember."

She rolled her eyes. "It's a wonder your ego can fit inside the building."

"That's why I built the biggest office space in the known universe."

"I don't like to beg."

"But I do enjoy watching you do it. From those pouty lips to impatient sighs and back again."

"Okay, I've had enough. Will you help or not? All I'm asking you to do is provide a location." Sitting up straight to fortify her defenses, she fired what she hoped was the winning salvo. "Let Reece make his own decisions."

"And therein lies the problem, my sweet Sarah. If I do what you want, I'm taking that choice away from him."

"So he doesn't have anyone else?"

"Not that I know of."

"Then maybe he still feels something for me."

"Now who has the ego?"

Hands open, she implored, "Just get him into the same place as me. All I want from him is one night."

"You're hoping to exorcise the demon? Prove he no longer matters to you?"

Maybe she'd built his memory into something of a shrine. No real man could live up to what she remembered. No one was that perfect.

"I always thought you were a bit more of a realist than that."

"For God's sake, Julien, just invite me to your birthday party."

"I haven't since you left Reece."

And she hated that. Julien threw himself spectacular parties. Even though the festivities were top secret, rumor had it that he'd rented a private island in the Florida Keys. He'd reportedly chartered ferries to shuttle his guests in. Even if she didn't have an ulterior motive, she would want to be there. "Are you intending to try to keep us apart for the rest of our lives? I never get invited to one of your events unless Reece stays away? Look, he can always refuse to see me." And if he did, she was sure there'd be plenty of other men there to help her drown her sorrows.

"He may be unkind. And by that, I mean an asshole like you've never seen. He has it in him."

"I'm prepared for that."

"He may want you to pay, get the revenge he's entitled to."

She shivered a little, and she wasn't sure whether it was from fear or from anticipation. At one time, when he'd stripped the clothes from her body, desire had beaded her nipples and made her tremble. "It will be all up to him," she said.

Julien remained silent, his eyebrows knotted in concentration.

"Reece deserves the opportunity to hear an explanation along with my apology."

"Are you hoping he'll beat you?"

"So you do know about that part of our relationship," she said, expelling her breath in relief.

"In vague terms. Bondage. Whips. Chains. Handcuffs." He swept his gaze over her body. "If that's what you're looking for, I'm happy to read a few books, buy a few things and tie you—"

"Stuff it, Julien. Not from you or anyone else." Except Reece. "We both know he would never touch me out of anger." She had complete confidence in that. "And I don't expect he'd actually agree to scene, but it's a possibility."

"And you still want to pursue your insane idea?"

"Yes."

Julien stretched out his legs and crossed them at the ankle. He tapped a finger against the rim of the expensive crystal glass.

"So you are going to help me?" She sighed in gratitude.

"Sweetling, there's nothing I enjoy more than meddling in

the affairs of others. The stickier and messier the better. I just wanted to hear the juicy details that Reece has so self-ishly kept to himself. And hearing you grovel for a bit was an added bonus."

"So this—"

"Strictly for my perverted entertainment."

"You're a bastard, Julien Bonds."

"Of the worst sort," he agreed.

CHAPTER ONE

What the fuck? Stunned, Reece McRae froze in place and stared at the woman prostrate before him.

Even though he couldn't see her face, there was no doubt that it was Sarah. His Sarah. The woman he'd planned to collar, marry, cherish for the rest of his days.

She wore a black corset that had a white arrow on each side, making her waist look impossibly tiny. A skirt covered her buttocks—barely—and hinted at exposed flesh beneath.

Though it had been two years since he'd seen her, Reece remembered every one of her delicious curves. He recalled how silky soft she'd felt as he'd skimmed his fingertips across her skin.

At one time, he'd grasped handfuls of her long hair. Now its length pooled onto the hardwood floor. Her arms were stretched in front of her, and her hands were on the floor, palms facing up.

She remained in position, waiting on his command. Her reappearance was as unwelcome as it was unwanted.

And, this close, the scent of her—femininity wrapped in

the musk of unrequited love and unexplored promise—wrapped around him and transported him back.

From the moment she'd walked into his company to apply for a job as his personal assistant four years before, he'd been attracted to her. After reminding himself that he had to be professional, he'd taken the time to consider all the applicants the human resources department had pre-screened. But she'd had the best résumé, and she'd interviewed better than anyone else.

Even on their first project, they'd thrived. They'd made one hell of a team. In a short time, he'd come to count on her brilliance, creativity and upbeat nature. He'd gone to the office every day with a smile.

At night, he'd hated saying goodbye. And he'd wanted, oh, so much more from her.

Though McRae International didn't have rules against fraternizing, as the CEO, he operated from his own set of guidelines. He didn't date employees. He compartmentalized each area of his life.

It had taken nearly four months to convince himself that going on a single date couldn't hurt. They'd worked late one night, and he'd invited her to dine with him afterwards. Instead of a quick bite, he'd taken her to his home and had grilled a couple of steaks. Though they'd shared an office suite, she'd kept her personal life cloaked in mystery. He'd never heard her make a phone call during the day, nor had he caught her spending any time on social media or answering anything other than company emails. It was as if she became a different person after she logged off the computer for the night. And the more time he'd spent with her, the more he'd wanted to know who the real Sarah was.

After dinner, he'd loaded the dishwasher, invited her to stay the night and promised her that he would be a complete gentleman. She had teased him about it. He'd admitted it

16

was, indeed, a rarity. He'd made up the guest room, and when she'd slipped past him, he'd touched her shoulder, and she'd paused.

He hadn't consciously planned to kiss her, but having her in his arms, that close, had melted his steely resolve.

And she'd responded to his kiss.

The next morning, while she'd slept, he'd gone for a long run around Memorial Park. He'd wondered what the hell he'd been thinking in bringing her home. Tasting Sarah had been like having a bite of dessert. She'd been decadent and delicious, and the sample had only increased his appetite. It —she—*they* were impossible on every level. He had sexual desires that were outside the norm. He'd scared off more than a handful of women over the years.

He'd gotten where he was in life by taking carefully calculated risks.

Seducing Sarah would be one of the worst ideas he'd ever had. After all, what were the chances that his perfect assistant would also want to be his kinky little submissive?

Finding a world-class employee was rare. He could find play partners. But over the next few weeks, the more he'd tried to deny the idea of being with her, the more it had persisted.

Behaving at work had become a bigger struggle each day.

His friend Julien had warned him of the dangers. If the relationship fell apart, Reece would be without a lover as well as a valuable work ally.

Reece had quickly discovered that, when it came to Sarah, logic was a thing of the past.

A month later, he'd asked her to accompany him to an after-hours business meeting. He'd rationalized that he could explain her presence to his associates, to her, even to himself. As if he'd still been a teenager, he'd held his breath until she'd agreed to be his guest.

In that moment, when she'd slipped into his car and he'd heard the whisper of her silk stockings and seen an expanse of thigh beneath her dress's hem, he'd known he had a difficult choice to make. Less than a week later, he'd done the only thing possible. He'd fired her and asked her to move in.

After her initial shock, she'd accepted. They'd celebrated their new life with a honeymoon of sorts. When they'd returned to Houston, she'd started her own business, working from the home they'd shared. Over the next year and a half, she'd become his most valued ally, his trusted advisor. He'd loved having her at business dinners and on trips. Every decision they'd made had supported their commitment to their growing relationship.

Or so he'd believed until he'd returned home from work one day to find the house, her home office and his life empty.

For the first few days after she'd run, he'd imagined turning her delectable ass every shade of red before welcoming her back into his arms and life...where she belonged.

Then reality had sent in.

She was never coming back.

After the anger and stunned disbelief had worn off—an embarrassingly long time later—he'd picked up the pieces of his shattered dreams and had stowed them, and the memory of her, away. Lesson driven home.

Now he told himself to turn the fuck around and go find Julien and slam his betraying ass against the wall, despite the fact that it was his birthday weekend. The man was no fool. He had known that Sarah was in the room when he'd told Reece he'd procured a lovely sub for an evening of entertainment.

More than anyone, Julien knew what Reece had been through. After all, he'd been with him the whole miserable way. Together with their friend Kennedy, they'd emptied a fair number of Scotch bottles. But Reece hadn't moved on. A month later, Julien had grown weary of Reece's moroseness and had staged an intervention. Julien had said that he'd tracked down Sarah. As he'd dumped expensive booze down the drain, he'd added that she was safe, but that she wanted to be left alone. Afterwards, he'd dragged Reece to the gym, forced him to work on business plans and re-engage in his life.

By even the harshest of standards, Reece had done well for himself.

But there was a reason for those sad songs on jukeboxes. Did one ever recover from the shock of losing one's soul mate?

She remained in position, gaze cast down, and he couldn't deny the attraction he still felt. His cock hardened, and he ached to slide inside her warmth.

To her credit, she'd learnt a few things in the two years since he'd seen her.

During their time together, he'd repeatedly told her how he wanted to be greeted. Submissively... By her waiting for her Master's pleasure. She'd always struggled with his request. She had no patience. So she'd either sneak a glance at him, giggle, talk incessantly or shift nervously.

But tonight she maintained the perfect position. Her forehead was pressed to the floor, and her long brown hair—kissed with sunshine-blonde highlights—had been swept to one side, leaving her nape exposed. Everything about her radiated vulnerability. Tonight she was behaving like the woman he'd always wanted her to be.

A frisson of jealousy gnawed at his spine. Who the hell had taught her the things she'd refused to learn from him?

Though he let the minutes drag, she didn't speak or fidget. Only her shortened breaths betrayed her nerves.

Truthfully, his silence wasn't a test for her. He was buying time, figuring out how to react, searching for places to file away his thoughts and reactions. Elation. Devastation. Curiosity. It would be stupid to open old wounds. But a greater, unhealed part wanted to know why the hell she'd left. What had scared her so bad that she hadn't been able to turn to him?

"Kneel up." His command was familiar. Her response was not.

Her movements were sensual, graceful as she unfolded her body then used abdominal strength to lift herself from the floor.

She positioned her knees wider than she'd ever been able to. With a gentle shrug, she pulled back her shoulders before linking her hands behind her head. As if she'd done it a thousand times, she shook her head. Her hair fell back from her face, and she met his gaze.

There was no shock etched between her eyebrows. Instead, her green eyes were open wide with trust.

She swallowed deeply and said nothing.

For a minute, he forgot how to breathe. As big and strong a corporate strategist that he was—accustomed to negotiations so tense they made front page news—he had just had his brains scrambled by a woman a bit under five feet tall.

She continued to look at him without blinking, seeming to offer Reece a glimpse of her soul.

He scoffed at the ridiculous thought. The man who'd been fanciful enough to believe that kind of romantic crap no longer existed. And the woman in front of him was the reason why. "You knew I'd be at this party?"

"Yes."

"Did you put Julien up to it? Or did he put you up to it?"

"It's my fault. I begged, cajoled, pleaded. Blame me."

"What the hell do you want, Sarah?"

She faltered then, looking down at the ground before

glancing back at him. But when she spoke, her words had a confidence that had been missing in the past. "To connect. Talk. Explain. Apologize."

Silence hung.

Then after a quick breath, she rushed on. "To scene."

"Why?"

"I'm hoping one night together will help me get over you."

He'd been expecting something else. Something more profound. As it was, he rocked back on his heels.

"I need to convince myself that what we had wasn't as good as I remember."

Reece searched her face, looking for...what? The truth? A hidden agenda? An answer to the dozens of unresolved questions?

"I'm hoping you'll indulge me with a beating, Sir."

Her courtesy was new, too. In all the time they'd been together, she'd called him Mr McRae at work and Reece at home. Even in a scene, she'd been unable to force herself to address him as Sir.

It wasn't until after she'd left that he had realized they hadn't been as close to his image of the perfect union as he would have liked.

"I've never found anyone like you, Sir."

"You've been looking?" The sense of betrayal that had simmered for years churned to a low boil. He now knew better than to stay near any woman who ignited that kind of emotion in him.

"Not consciously. No."

"But?" he prompted.

"I've compared everyone else to you. How could I not?" She hesitated, as if reluctant to say more. "I've never connected with anyone like I did with you. No one compares with you. I'm...frustrated, I guess."

"If nothing else, I owe you an explanation," she said, her

21

voice strong as well as melodious and mysterious. She took a deep breath. "And I need to apologize."

"Save your breath. I won't accept it." Not now.

Sarah winced.

He turned and strode toward the door instead of succumbing to temptation and sweeping her into his arms.

"Sir?"

He paused but didn't look back at her.

"I deserve your anger. Your hostility. But I was hoping for more than your indifference. You know that's the thing I fear the most. The way you're capable of cutting people off, emotionally and physically."

She was right about that.

"I don't give second chances," he reminded her. But indifference toward her? When she was so utterly beautiful and had yanked out a part of his heart when she'd run? Not likely.

But had that been part of the problem? The fact that he'd always been so available to her? Besotted had been the horrifying word Julien had used.

"We shared something special." Undeterred, she persisted, "Surely you've wanted to beat some sense into me? Punish me, maybe, for the way I left?"

"I imagined it," he conceded. "But that was a long time ago. Don't fool yourself that I even think of you anymore."

He heard her take a shaky breath before saying, "I know I don't deserve your forgiveness, so I won't ask for it. But I'm begging you to show some mercy. Let me atone."

Her plea sliced through his defenses.

Despite his best intentions, he faced her. *Fuck.* What the hell was it about her? He wanted to pretend that sexual attraction didn't exist between them, but it was there, raw, primal, pulsing. This woman could lead him around by his dick.

He reminded himself that she'd given him, them, no chance at success or a future. Part of him hated her for that, her cowardice, for not being the woman he'd wanted.

"Reece… Sir…"

"Nice manners," he said.

"Thank you, Sir."

"If you're still in this room in sixty seconds, you'll get everything you're asking for."

The woman at his feet wore no makeup, hid behind no artifice. "I'm not running."

"This time."

Her head snapped back to indicate his direct hit. But then, even more forcefully, she repeated, "I'm not running."

"You should."

"I'm sure you're right."

His beautiful, stubborn former lover remained in place.

"I don't know whether to applaud your bravery or condemn your stupidity," he said.

"Perhaps both, Sir." She attempted a smile that fell flat. "Internally I'm doing both right now."

He remembered hearing the same mixture of anticipation and nerves in her voice the first night he'd tied her hands to his headboard. He'd treated her as if she were the most delicate, precious thing—and to him, she had been.

But her callousness had changed him, hardened him.

"Scene with me, Sir?"

"Not a chance."

"Julien tells me you don't have a sub right now. Surely you miss that, if nothing else?"

He did. It had been a long time since he'd played with a submissive, and Julien knew it. "The room setup," he said, glancing around. "You or Julien?"

"Julien."

He nodded. While Reece preferred suspension, the St

Andrew's cross that Julien had provided was large and sturdy with thick leather cuffs, perfect for securing even the biggest, strongest, most recalcitrant sub.

"I understand he had it built here by a local carpenter."

Were they that sure of his reaction? Or of his lunacy where she was concerned?

"Your toy bag is over there." She inclined her head.

"Adding breaking and entering to your résumé, Ms Lovett?"

"No, Sir. Julien has a key," she reminded him.

"Ah. The letter of the law versus the spirit of the law argument."

"The ends justify the means," she said with a grin.

His resolve wavered. He'd rarely been able to deny this woman anything. More than anyone, she knew his weaknesses. "Did you thoughtfully provide him instructions on what to include?"

She remained silent.

"A cane, perhaps?"

If the way her shoulders rolled forward was any indication, bravado had momentarily fled.

"Rattan was made for you," he said.

"If you say so, Sir."

"But I'm betting there's not a cane in the bag."

"It was too big, Sir."

"And the crop, as well."

She nodded. "Much too long, Sir."

"As I thought. So you had Julien provide only the implements you wanted," he said.

Silence damned her.

He'd barely introduced her to the cane's sear before she'd left. He'd used a crop on her a handful of times, and she hadn't objected too much to the taste of its flapper on her nipples. But when he'd flicked the leather across her swollen pussy, she'd screamed, then exhaled in a shud-dering orgasm. The memory drained the blood from his brain.

It was insanity to stay in the room with her. He could return to the main party area and enjoy a lap dance from one of the 'guests' Julien had invited for entertainment purposes.

"You're wondering what's in the bag," Sarah said.

Now I am.

He looked down at her. She had to be uncomfortable by now, but she hadn't fidgeted or complained. Another new thing. "Fetch it."

With a grace that had escaped her years ago, she rose and crossed to the corner.

She picked up the canvas bag and carried it to him. She stopped inches from him, close enough that he was undone by her presence. He'd been unaware of the hint of vanilla that mingled with her womanly aroma. Now it consumed him. "Tell me what's in there," he said, surprised that his tongue still worked and that he could form words.

"A small whip."

He knew from the shape of the bag that there were a few other items. "And?" he prompted. The longer he stood in front of her, the more the conversation wound him in, the more he knew he was helpless to resist her.

"And two of your fifty-strand floggers."

"Which two?"

With a boldness he'd never seen in her, she looked up at him.

"I asked Julien to pick the red one. In the past you told me how much you liked the way the strands matched the marks you left on my back."

He suddenly felt like a fish. Not just because his mouth was open, but because he knew how close he was to going for the bait she was sexily dangling in front of him.

"I also suggested he add the looped one you'd planned to use in public with me."

"The same night nerves overcame you and you needed to stay home?"

"I'm much braver now," she said.

"Are you?" Too bad they wouldn't have the opportunity to test her promise.

"There are also assorted paddles, several pairs of clamps, lube, a vibrator…" She faltered before continuing, "Ah, a hood."

"Which you refused to wear in the past."

"I told you I'm braver now." She continued to meet his gaze. "I also included bondage tape."

"Quite thorough." And designed to pique his interest. "I imagine Julien enjoyed his forage through my private things."

"He said he did, Sir." She grinned. "He thoughtfully included an entire box of condoms. Assorted colors and flavors. Ribbed and smooth. I told him that was fine, as long as he bought you the giant-sized ones."

Suddenly he wondered at the conversations the two had shared.

"I assured him I would take all the blame."

"I'm happy to give it all to you."

Goosebumps chased up her bare arms.

"Fear?" he asked.

"A little," she confessed.

"Good."

"I won't change my mind. I'm nervous, not scared. There's a difference."

"Put down the bag."

She set it at his feet.

He noticed her hesitation then. He helped her out. "Kneel." When she did, he added, "Choose three items from it."

Time and silence merged and dragged until the sound of her shuddered sigh broke the quiet.

"You can leave any time," he said, needing to say something that reminded them both that he was in charge.

In answer, she unzipped the bag. The first thing she selected was a pair of soft handcuffs.

He accepted them, telling himself that he didn't notice the gentle drag of her nails on his palm and that nerve endings hadn't sparked in response.

She then selected the red flogger.

He accepted it, as well. "And finally?"

She rooted through the contents and pulled out a silk scarf.

"Excellent choices."

"Thank you, Sir," she said, smiling up at him.

"Now put them back."

Her smile faded. "Sir?"

"You've got one more chance."

She shuddered.

"All this is your choice," he reminded her. "From the elaborate ruse, to the well-equipped play space. So if you want the beating you say you crave, entice me."

Reece wanted to scare her. He wanted her to have second, third, fourth thoughts about moving forward. He wanted her to run for the door so that he could prove they weren't right for each other.

For less than a heartbeat, she hesitated. Then she took each item from him and dropped them into the bag. Her lack of care with his belongings told him that he'd made her nervous.

This time, the first thing she pulled out was a pair of nipple clamps.

He nodded and accepted them.

Then she gave him a blindfold.

"Very good," he said. "And what will you select next?"

Both of her hands were inside the bag, and she was looking in its depths. With a deep sigh, she removed his favorite flogger. The strands were looped, giving it an entirely different feel from the red one. It was beefier and had more oomph. "Well done, Sarah."

"Thank you, Sir."

He realized how important his approval really was to her, and how much deeper he was getting pulled in with each moment. "Now put on the nipple clamps."

"I... I don't understand."

Of course she didn't. On the few times she'd been adorned with them, he'd affixed them, after a lot of play and a certain amount of distraction. And she was still dressed.

"You'll need to loosen my corset," she said.

"I'll find someone else to do it."

"What? Are you out of your mind?"

"Or we can call it a night, go and have a drink at the bar. Catch up on the last couple of years."

"Fine. Go ahead and find someone else to loosen it."

He placed her selections on a banquet table before heading into the hallway. A young couple were walking toward him. From the way they were leaning on each other and the way she was giggling at something he'd said, it appeared that they were already having a great time. "Do you mind giving me a hand with my lady's corset?"

The couple looked at each other. "Why not?" the woman said with a shrug. "They can be tricky."

"How do you know that, luvie?" the gentleman asked.

"I have one or two."

"All kinds of secrets you're keeping, Magenta."

"You'll never know," she replied with a cheeky flip of her hair.

"I'm intrigued." To Reece he added, "Ten years together and she can still surprise me."

The woman walked to where Sarah stood.

"Men are helpless at these things," Magenta said.

"Indeed we are," Reece agreed.

Sarah glared at him. "Only when it suits you."

"Indeed." He'd cinched her into one and slowly released her at least a dozen times in the past. "You're welcome to put a stop to it at any time."

In answer, she turned her back to them.

"Quite the kinky setup you've got here," Magenta's companion said. "Ah… Terribly rude of me." He extended a hand. "Name's North Star."

"A pseudonym, I take it," Reece said.

"Left the real world behind on the mainland," he answered.

They shook hands. "Reece McRae."

"I've heard of you."

"God," Sarah choked out. "Seriously?"

"Mind if we have a go after you're finished in here?" the man asked.

"Wait a minute," Magenta said. "You're not getting me up on that thing."

"No, love," North Star agreed. "I was more thinking that I'd let you tie me up to it and have your wicked way with me."

"In that case, I'm very interested."

While Magenta loosened the laces, Reece exchanged telephone numbers with North Star.

"You'll text me as soon as you're finished?"

"It's a private room that Julien set up. You're welcome to use it, but don't broadcast its existence."

"Fair enough."

"All done," Magenta announced. "We'll give you some privacy now."

As the two exited, Sarah turned back to face him, holding the corset in place. The door closed, and the sudden silence seemed to ricochet. "Lower it," he instructed.

Slowly, she did.

"Gorgeous," he said. He remembered her being beautiful, but he hadn't remembered just what kind of impact she had on him.

He reached out and took the leather from her. "Now the skirt."

"I should have expected that."

"Yes. You should have."

She lowered the zipper then shimmied from the material, letting it fall to the floor.

"You're sexy as ever, Sarah."

"I—"

"You're perfect."

She'd put on a couple of pounds since he'd seen her last, and it suited her, filled her out, made her all the more soft and feminine. One night? It would never be enough.

"You make me feel that way," she said.

"You are. Now the panties. And whatever made you think it would be okay to wear them?"

She blushed then, reminding him of the innocent she'd once been.

"That was remiss."

"Do you remember what the penalty used to be?"

"Penalty?"

"Don't be coy."

"Ten stripes with whatever implement you chose."

"And your favorite was?"

"Your hand, Sir."

Careful, his common sense warned. This Sarah, innocent, charming, would be his undoing. "Take them off."

"You used to cut them off me."

"Not tonight. Leave the shoes on." They made her legs impossibly long and showed off her calves. And he was, after all, only a man.

If she had been performing a striptease, she couldn't have taken more time. She wriggled as she drew the silk scrap of material over her hips, exposing her nicely trimmed patch of hair. She still wore it exactly as he'd once instructed. Either that, or she'd intentionally done it, just for him. Regardless, it tantalized and melted another part of his cold resolve.

Her gaze on him, she slid her panties down her thighs.

She reached for his forearm to steady herself as she worked them off over her heels.

"Good," he told her when she stood up straight. He removed her hand. "Now the clamps." He crossed to the table near the door, grateful for the momentary distance. If he'd hoped that time would have diminished her hold on him, he'd been wrong. He snatched up the metal chain and carried the set to her.

Softly, she said, "I'd appreciate it if you'd do it for me."

A hundred times, *yes*. "No."

"Is this some sort of test?"

"It is."

"You want to scare me off, make me go away so you can absolve yourself of any responsibility."

"Maybe." He dangled the chain over his forefinger. "Put them on or not."

She pinched each nipple in turn. Then, in that intentionally sensual way, she brushed her fingers over his. He squared his shoulders and remained stoic.

"This is more difficult than it looks," she said.

"I'm sure it is."

She placed the clamps with two small hisses. After exhaling, she shook out her hair and pulled back her shoulders.

"Been a long time?"

"Yes, Sir."

He glanced away to hide his quick, triumphant grin. The knowledge that she hadn't been playing with others, at least not recently, pleased him. Before he lost his brain entirely, he looked at her and asked, "What's your safe word?"

"I haven't changed it. It's the same as it's always been."

"Remind me."

She shivered, as if his response had shocked and chilled her. "Cream pie."

He had never forgotten. More than three years ago, at an annual presentation to shareholders, a pissed-off former employee had busted through the meeting room doors and thrown a pie at him. Reece had removed his jacket, used it to wipe off his face, then had turned back his cuffs and continued the meeting while security had subdued the man.

When the assailant had gone to court, Reece had testified on the man's behalf. Reece had persuaded the judge to allow the man to perform community service rather than go to jail. Later, as they'd showered together at home, Sarah had confessed to being impressed by his reaction. If he could be so restrained when it came to someone he didn't like, he was unlikely to overreact when it came to dealing with her.

"I know you remember."

He closed his hand around the chain of her clamps.

In a low, quiet, soft voice, she added, "I trust you, Reece."

"Until you walked out, I would have said that was a smart decision."

"Now you're not as sure?"

No one had ever inflamed such a combustible mixture of emotional angst inside him. "You'd be smart to change your mind."

"I won't."

He nodded. "Cream pie it is." He tugged on the chain.

She remained in place and closed her eyes against the pain. He pulled her toward him. She swayed.

"How do you like it?" he asked.

"Fine."

"Then open your eyes and tell me."

"I like it fine, Sir. Thank you."

"And now?" He tightened his grip.

"Even better."

"Little liar." He uncurled his fist. "If I can't trust you to be honest, we're done."

"You misunderstand." She shook her head. "It wasn't dishonest in the least. I've missed this. Want it."

He welcomed this new, more expressive side of her personality. "You may walk to the cross any time you wish," he said as he dropped the metal.

Under normal circumstances, he'd run his fingers over her skin, tip back her head, offer a kiss or words of encouragement. Instead, he folded his arms across his chest.

Honestly, part of him wished she'd give in to a case of the nerves and flee from the room. "Any time you're ready," he said, indicating the cross.

She drew a breath. "I am."

The sound of her heels was all but silent on the carpet. The sight of her walking, the sway of her hips, the flex of her calf muscles, the expanse of her back all caused an earthquake of emotion in him.

As she spread her arms and her legs, he went to the table and palmed the blindfold. Then he attached the cowhide flogger to his belt loop.

"I'm going to put on your blindfold."

She nodded.

"No protests?"

"I'm your perfect submissive, Sir."

He shook his head. "Did you say that with a straight face?"

"No. But I tried."

The gentleness, the teasing reminded him of another time, another place, before her actions had poisoned their love affair.

He walked around so that he could place the blindfold on her. Then he stepped back and looked at her. Unlike times in the past, she remained still.

The woman before him had an air of tranquility about her that he'd never seen.

"How do the nipple clamps feel?"

"Perfect," she responded. "Because I know they please you."

In that moment, he realized he was under her spell. "I want you to hold onto the wrist straps," he said.

"You're not binding me?"

"No. I want you to clearly understand that you're free to walk away at any time."

"That's fine. I'm happy with you knowing that I'm staying. Of my own free will."

He squeezed her breasts. Her moan was one of pleasure, and she leaned into the cross and him.

"Please beat me, Sir," she invited. "Unless that was too bold?"

"Just the opposite," he told her. He appreciated her words, the plea that was threaded through them. "It was perfect."

He went to stand behind her then unclipped the flogger. This wasn't a flogger for a sustained erotic beating, it was too mean for that.

Wanting to arouse her senses, he draped the strands over her shoulders. Then he rubbed her legs, buttocks and back lightly.

He skimmed his fingers up the inside of her thighs, but he didn't touch her pussy.

"Yes, Sir," she said softly.

Her words were husky, letting him know she was starting to slip into a more submissive mindset.

For a couple of minutes, he worked on her thighs and buttocks, massaging vigorously, giving her a few swats. "Are you warmed up?"

"That was only a warm-up?" she asked. Then, instead of saying anything else, she gripped the restraints tighter, silently letting him know she was ready.

"Hold on," he warned her, picking up the flogger and taking two steps back.

"Yes, Sir."

He caught the underside of her buttocks.

Her breath whooshed out.

A thick red mark appeared, and a feeling of possessiveness seared him. Its intensity shocked him. He was sure he'd moved past there where she was concerned.

He hit her again, this time with more force, lifting her onto her toes.

"Needed this," she murmured.

Reece used the flogger again, scorching her upper thighs.

She hissed, but remained in perfect position, legs apart, her hands on the restraints. "More," she said.

"Greedy sub."

"Yes, Sir."

When they had been lovers, partners, he had taken the time to ensure her sexual arousal. Reece had never beaten her for punishment, nor would he start now. He'd crafted scenes solely for her erotic pleasure. And sometimes he'd given her several orgasms a night.

This time, however, he used a slow, measured pace. It was

sure to arouse her, but not satisfy her. He took great pleasure in that.

He had forced her onto her toes and his strokes kept her there.

Her buttocks turned a beautiful shade of red, and his cock hardened in response.

Reece made the tenth stroke his most powerful, and she screamed. Her knees buckled. Reece dropped the flogger and caught her. He took her shoulders and turned her, gathering her body against his.

In all of her appealing softness, disheveled hair, and damp cheeks, she accepted his comfort, burrowing her head against his shoulder as she shook.

"Shh." He smoothed the silken strands and held her close, where she'd once fitted so perfectly, where he'd dreamt she always belonged.

In his arms, she was so small, seemed so vulnerable, incapable of inflicting the harm that she'd caused.

"You haven't lost your touch," she told him.

"I'm glad you approve." Once he was sure that her legs were steady, he released her and took a step back. "How are you doing?"

"A little shaky," she confessed. "Like I said, it's been a long time."

"Did it hurt worse than you remember?"

"Physically?" She met his gaze. "No. But this used to bring us closer. And I feel as if there's a huge wedge between us."

"There is." Reece imagined that he could swim in the clear, honest, green depths of her eyes. He almost laughed at the ridiculousness of the idea. Whoever had said that the eyes were the window of the soul had been wrong. The night before she'd left, she'd looked at him and told him she loved him. Now, just like then, her eyes were wide, guileless. This was a woman who could lie to him without blinking. He'd do well to remember that.

"I wish…"

"Leave it, Sarah." Clearly she longed for an orgasm. And if he lost his focus, he'd give her one. "Let's get the clamps off you."

"I sort of hate that worse than having them put on."

"Would you rather do it yourself?"

She looked up at him. "No."

He removed the first then took her nipple into his mouth, sucking until she reached for his shoulders. Then he did the same for her other nipple.

"Thank you," she said.

"I was sure you were going to remember your manners," he said.

"Better late than never?" she asked.

He pocketed the clamps before removing his shirt. He put it on her and buttoned it up. In the past, they'd often helped each other dress. It surprised him how naturally they'd fallen back into the habit. "Julien can arrange to have the room cleaned."

She looked up at him, her head tipped back, the column of her throat exposed to him. He remembered the day he'd bought her engagement ring and the afternoon her collar had been delivered to his office. And he recalled the day she'd vanished without a fucking word.

He'd thought he'd moved past the hurt, but he hadn't. He'd only buried it. And now it was back, raw and biting. Suddenly he wanted answers, and he wouldn't be satisfied without them. "We're going to talk. I'll give you thirty minutes to freshen up. Then meet me at the Coral Reef. If you're not there, you won't like the consequences. This time, Sarah, there's nowhere for you to run. Nowhere for you to hide."

CHAPTER TWO

Sarah shivered.

Needing to protect herself, she crossed her arms over her chest.

"Did you hear me?"

"I did," she said.

He tapped a finger on her chest, and the sensation reverberated through her.

"Yes, Sir," she whispered. Maybe this hadn't been one of her better ideas. Part of her had actually believed that sceneing with him would help her get over him. Instead, it had made things worse.

In the years since she'd left him, she'd forgotten how masterful he was. But the moment the flogger's strands had kissed her skin, the memories had flooded back. She'd remembered everything, from the first time he'd undressed her, to the first time he'd caressed her, to the first time he'd squeezed her buttocks before blazing her skin with his hand.

As she'd stood there, bound to the cross by her own volition, she'd again given herself over to him, knowing he would care for her. But she'd been unprepared for the way he had overwhelmed her senses.

When he'd entered the room earlier, she'd known it was him, even though she hadn't been able to see anything and he hadn't spoken. The forceful sound of the door slamming had ignited her nerve endings.

She'd wanted to look at him, drink in his tall, good looks. Remaining still had taken all of her resolve.

When he'd instructed her to kneel up, she'd been breathless.

The years they'd been apart had hardened him. Either that, or it was just her who brought out the steel in his eyes, in the rigidity of his posture.

No matter what, he still devastated her.

Standing in front of him, close enough that every one of her breaths was scorched by his scent, she yearned to run her fingers over his chest or bury them in his thick, dark hair. Her pussy throbbed with the need for his touch.

Always, he'd made her climax during or immediately following a scene. She keenly felt the absence of his touch.

Sarah had told Julien, and herself, that she knew what she was doing. Now, with Reece standing so close, and her being all but naked, she wasn't so sure.

Until this moment, she'd underestimated his power over her. She'd been right to run. This man, more than any other, made her aware of her femininity and vulnerability. Before she was ready, he scooped her from the floor, into his arms.

"What are you doing?" she demanded.

"Taking you back to your room. You're not traipsing through the resort half dressed."

"I wasn't wearing much more than this when I walked down here," she reminded him.

He was already striding toward the door when he said, "Non-negotiable, Ms Lovett."

His tone was curt. When he was like that, she knew better than to continue the argument. Instead, she sighed and wrapped an arm around his neck "I need my purse, Reece." She pointed to a small clutch on a table.

He carried her to fetch it.

"This is ridiculous," she said as she snatched up the bag. "It would be easier if you let me walk."

"What's your room number?"

She realized he wasn't going to respond to her statement. "Nine twelve."

"Not a surprise. I'm on the ninth floor, as well."

"Julien has a hand in everything," she said.

Reece carried her from the meeting room and through the hotel's lobby. She would have died from embarrassment except for the fact that there were women who were showing way more body parts than she was.

At the bank of elevators, Reece juggled her against his chest in order to push the call button.

Julien and an entourage, two bodyguards and five women, were walking through the lobby toward one of the bars.

He stopped but waved, indicating that the others should continue on. A bodyguard hovered nearby while the other herded the women toward the reverberating beat of a steel drum.

As always, Julien made an impression. His suit looked casual, but the cut emphasized his lean mass. He had left the top button of his white shirt open. He hadn't shaved for at least a day and on him, the stubble was sexy, sexy. That he wasn't surrounded by more than five women only meant that the evening was young.

"Judging by the fact you both seem to have lost some articles of clothing, I'd say the two of you have found you still have something in common," he observed.

"I won't thank you for meddling," Reece said.

Despite his words, he tightened his grip on her, and he eased her closer to his body.

"Of course you will," Julien said. Then he addressed Sarah. "I take it your plan didn't work?"

A hot blush stung her cheeks.

"Plan?" Reece asked.

"Sarah wanted to exorcise the hold you had on her. I think you both owe me your everlasting gratitude. And, Reece, feel free to tell Kennedy to throw me a few hundred shares of the next company you're going to take public. We can consider it a thank you as well as a birthday present. I know I'm difficult to shop for."

"Piss up a rope."

"Meet me on the basketball court in the morning. We'll settle this like men."

"Fair enough. And send someone to clean up the room."

Julien nodded to the security guard who spoke into a microphone attached to his lapel.

The elevator dinged its arrival.

"Since you apparently have unfinished business, I'll forgive you if you're not at any of tonight's activities," Julien said. "But I fully expect both of you at my official party tomorrow night. Oh, and Reece, you may want to buy your woman some underwear." He winked at her before moving off with his bodyguard.

Eyes narrowed, Reece glanced down at her.

"He was messing with you," she told him. "This shirt is long enough that no one can see anything."

He remained silent but carried her into the car and pushed the button for their floor.

"You can put me down now," she said.

In response, he gave her a quick pinch.

"Ouch! Reece…" She wasn't sure if she was protesting or

saying thanks. Honestly she wanted to stay where she was. His strength gave her an odd sense of comfort.

In front of her door, he finally let her go. He took the key card from her and inserted it in the electronic reader before turning the handle to open the door.

"The Coral Reef," he reminded her. "Thirty minutes. And be dressed in some decent clothes."

With that, he left her.

Having no other choice, she went inside.

The air-conditioned coolness was a blessed relief, and she sank onto the edge of the bed, shaking. A couple of weeks ago, when she'd first had this idea, everything had seemed easy enough. She'd see him, scene, apologize, put everything to rest, and go back to her everyday life, having filed the past away, where it belonged. But things seemed to be getting more tangled with each minute.

Playtime hadn't gone as she'd planned. In fact, she now had a good deal of sexual frustration woven alongside her doubts and questions.

The Reece who'd just carried her to her room wasn't the same man who'd entered the meeting room. He'd gone from not wanting to touch her to a fiery Dominant. This man was also different than he had been two years ago. That much was inevitable, she assumed. They'd both grown and changed.

At one time there'd been a light in his eyes when he'd looked at her, a softness in his voice when he'd spoken to her. Even when he'd given her orders, there had been an undercurrent that had reassured her of his love. But now…? Her hands shook from the attack of nerves.

If she were smart, she'd enlist Julien's help in getting off the island.

Yet she'd promised herself, and him, that she was no

longer the type of woman who ran. They could talk, have dinner then part in a friendly way. Nice and tidy.

But that idea didn't take into account the marks on her back or her twisted insides.

It was unusual for him to leave her alone after a scene. He never had before. Angst churned inside her.

Frustrated on all levels, she went into the bathroom, unbuttoned his shirt and shrugged it from her shoulders. For a few seconds, she held the lightweight material against her nose and breathed in the scent of him—expectation, determination and a warm, tropical breeze.

Telling herself that she was being fanciful, she dropped the garment, letting it pool onto the floor. Then she realized she hadn't been fanciful. The same scent clung to her skin. It was as familiar as her own name.

She turned and caught sight of a welt on her backside. The beating had barely been an appetizer. She was horny, and she wanted him.

Damn it.

Sarah stepped beneath the shower's spray, rested her forehead against the tile, closed her eyes then slid her hand between her legs.

Recalling the image of the flogger in Reece's strong hand, she rubbed her forefinger across her clit. Then she reimagined the jolt from the first strike. No matter how much she was expecting the impact, the first stroke always caught her somewhat off guard. This time it had been magnified by the fact that it had been so long since she'd scened with him.

Until he'd had her reach for the straps, she hadn't been sure that he'd even play with her. That emotional uncertainty had added to the nerves holding her rigid.

The delicious, biting caress of fifty leather strands on her bare skin had brought tears to her eyes, but only partially from the pain. For weeks, she'd been fantasizing, hoping, wishing that she could be with him again. Then, when it had happened, she'd been overcome with joy and relief.

That the lashes had been delivered by the only man she'd ever loved had been divine.

Sarah rubbed her clitoris faster and faster.

Her knees wobbled as the orgasm built. How had she ever thought life would be okay without Reece? And, worse, how had she let herself believe that one scene with him would help her to forget him?

When the hell had she become a master of self-deception?

With her left hand, she pinched her right nipple. The physical spike of endorphins from the momentary pain was all she needed, and she cried out his name as she orgasmed.

For a few minutes she stayed there, until she could stand up and draw a full breath.

She soaped her body and rinsed off in cool water, hoping that she'd look more collected than she felt when she met Reece.

She was still in the bathroom, wrapped in a towel, when she heard a knock on the door.

Her heart leaped, and she was half worried, half hoping that Reece had come looking for her.

Instead, a smiling housekeeper held her skirt, corset and thong. As always, Julien had gotten results. Sarah thanked the woman, gave her a tip then checked the time.

Realizing she had to hurry in order to not keep Reece waiting, she dumped the pile of clothes on the bed then dropped the towel on the floor. She reached for a lacy bra while she debated what to do about the panties. Reece had chastised her for wearing them. But then he'd been offended when Julien had pointed out her lack of underwear.

It probably didn't matter, she thought as she wriggled her slightly damp body into a pair of boy shorts. Reece had seen her naked and had obviously not been tempted. That she'd had to take care of her own orgasm stung much more than his whip had. The approving note in his voice when she'd removed the corset had given her hope. But he had avoided her pussy when he'd run his fingers up the inside of her thighs. When he'd sucked on her nipples, her expectations had soared. But since he hadn't touched her and he had passed up an unspoken invitation to fuck her, she suspected that he'd never know what she wore next to her skin.

She stepped into a long, flowing sundress and put on a pair of sandals. After piling her hair on top of her head and securing it with a clip, she applied a coat of mascara. Remembering that he was a fan of red lipstick, she wore that, too.

Realizing she'd used up every second of her allotted time, Sarah grabbed a shawl and her purse then headed toward the elevator.

The doors slid open, and there were at least a dozen people crammed into the car. "I'll wait for the next one," she said.

"Get in!" a man shouted from the back. "We'll make room."

She squeezed in. Moon Dog or Night Angels, whatever his name was, stood off to the side. His companion had her hand curled around his wrist.

"We wanted to say thanks. Your man let us know the room was available," he said.

She started to protest that Reece wasn't hers, but he went on, "He said we could use the cross but not any of the toys. Those are for you."

That surprised her and made her smile.

The elevator stopped on the eighth floor and, incredibly, two more revelers edged in, creating a loud party atmosphere.

"You're welcome to join us, have Reece show us a few things," Magenta added as they reached the first floor.

"I'll be sure to let him know." She gave a false, cheery smile before exiting and walking across the lobby.

Outside, humidity drenched the evening air. Noise from the hotel faded into the background. Potted plants lined the sidewalk, and a few palm trees swayed in the light breeze.

As she neared the restaurant entrance, she saw Reece.

He was waiting in the shadows, shoulders against the stucco wall. Her heart stuttered before surging on, thundering in her throat.

The image of him, larger than life, masculine and powerful, transported her four years into the past. She recalled the first time she'd seen him, when she'd walked into his office to interview for the job as his assistant. She'd clutched the handle of her briefcase so hard that her fingers had gone numb.

When he'd stood to greet her, the physical attraction she'd felt for him had unnerved her. Then he'd shaken her hand. She'd been so captivated by his blue eyes and dark good looks that she'd stammered over her own name.

It had taken more than a few minutes for her to relax and for him to focus. He'd seemed distracted with a pile of papers stacked on his desk. His shoulders had been rigid, his demeanor uninviting. In response, she'd perched on the edge of her chair.

It wasn't until he'd answered a call and knocked over a pile of manila folders that things had changed. While he'd continued his conversation, she'd cleaned up the mess, scanning each piece of paper to ensure that it was returned to the right place.

With a curt nod, he'd acknowledged her help.

Then he'd scowled as he'd listened to the person on the other end of the phone. She'd heard him use the word

DeVane, and since she'd seen that file, she had grabbed it, opened it and put it in front of him.

Without looking up, he'd shuffled through the papers, scanned a few of them, given her a thumbs-up and never lost his place in the conversation.

"Well done," he'd told her when he had hung up.

His approval had tripped through her, heating her. He'd added that he'd never worked so seamlessly with someone before. The rest of the interview had gone well. She'd been surprised and disappointed that he hadn't offered her a job right away, but she'd respected the way he'd informed her that he had another few candidates to consider and that he was obligated to follow HR's hiring protocol.

She'd wondered if he'd experienced the same chemical reaction, but had then chastised herself for being fanciful. Pictures of him were often featured on page three of the *Houston Enterprise.* In each, he had a beautiful, accomplished woman with him. He could have his pick of anyone. So why would he be interested in her?

But he had been.

To the point where he'd almost consumed her.

One hour in a private room with him had put her back in that same state. She was thinking about no one but him. This man dominated her thoughts along with her body.

"Good evening, Sarah," he said, taking her hand and raising it to his lips.

His old-world charm had always undone her. "Reece," she said.

"You look lovely."

She knew his compliment was sincere. As she'd learnt, he never said anything he didn't believe.

"You're wearing panties?"

Despite the heat, she shivered. "I am."

"Again, that's remiss of you."

"I had no idea it mattered to you."

"It does."

Even in the fading darkness, she felt the power of his gaze and heard the tension in his tone.

He gripped her shoulders and maneuvered her so that her back was to the wall. Her insides turned molten.

Reece McRae overwhelmed, consumed her.

Hungrily he slanted his mouth across hers.

Helpless, she linked her arms around his neck. As he demanded entrance to her mouth, she yielded.

His tongue met hers, and she tasted his passion. This was the man who'd captured her heart as well as her body so many years ago. And it was a reminder of why she'd run. When she was this close, her brain function shut down. All that remained were her base needs. She'd do anything, surrender everything.

His cock pressed against her. That he desired her with the same ferocity that she felt for him gave her a heady thrill.

With his tongue, he fucked her mouth, taking her as she'd hoped he would earlier in the meeting room.

"You're as responsive as always, Sarah," he said after ending the kiss and easing back a fraction of an inch.

"Only for you, Reece."

He rained kisses down the column of her throat, reminding her of the time that he'd loved her so completely.

"I meant it when I said I haven't met anyone your equal." Even though she'd taken care of herself a little while ago, his touch aroused her again. "You know I wasn't satisfied after that beating. It was…"

He wanted to know.

"Exquisite."

"Any bruises?"

She shook her head. "I was hopeful that I'd have one or two as a reminder. But no. Even the one red mark faded."

"I should put some knots in the end of the tails."

"Sounds...wicked."

"It can be." He took her chin and tipped her head back a notch. "Did you masturbate when you went to your room?" he asked.

"Yes. I did." She paused. "I was wound up. Lonely. Restless. I hadn't realized how much I would miss the aftercare you used to give me."

"It wasn't just one thing you walked away from."

"Intimacy," she said. And that was the first time she'd made the connection. What they'd shared had been deep on so many levels. And the way he'd spend twenty minutes with her after they'd scened had deepened the emotional connection. Sometimes he'd silently hold her. Or they'd talk about business. But he'd always taken time to be there for her, no matter what she'd needed.

"Shall we?" he asked.

Without waiting for her response, he placed his fingers on the small of her back and guided her toward the entrance. The tension that had been simmering heated up.

Possessiveness from this man felt like the right thing.

The maître d' greeted Reece warmly and led them away from the rest of the guests. He ushered them around a number of potted palms to a secluded table at the edge of the patio. A hedge of sorts served as a natural fence. A number of plants provided an array of color across the space. Even though it was still fairly light out, a candle flickered in the middle of the small table next to a tiny vase with a couple of neon pink blooms in it.

The maître d' pulled out her chair. Then, with a flick of his wrist, he draped her napkin across her lap.

"May I?" he asked, indicating the bottle of wine that was already waiting.

"Please," Reece said. After the man poured a small

amount, Reece tasted the white wine and nodded his approval.

The man poured two glasses before excusing himself.

"Nice service," she said.

"Julien wanted to be sure we enjoyed the evening."

"When did you plan this out?"

"I made a couple of phone calls while you were getting changed."

"He didn't leave menus."

"I took the liberty of arranging the meal."

"Of course you did." During the years they'd been together, they'd made a habit of exploring new foods and trying new wines to pair them with. "That's what Doms do."

"Are you displeased?"

"On the contrary."

"You've found others to do that for you, surely?"

"Anyone can ask what I want and convey my order to the wait staff. You were different. You took the time to learn about me. You knew my tastes as well as I did."

"That's not what I asked."

"No," she said. "No one else has paid the kind of attention to me that you do. I've missed it. I've missed you."

Reece picked up his glass and raised it in her direction. She did the same.

"To old friends," he said as they clinked their glasses together.

Stung, she took a sip. What had she expected? That he'd respond to her honesty with a wild profession of love? Devotion, maybe? Perhaps the on-his-knees confession that he couldn't wait to take her to bed and annihilate the tension in her tummy?

"How's the wine?"

Tasteless. This was the conversation of acquaintances, not lovers. "Fine."

"You went to great effort to seek me out, and I've decided to hear you out. I want to understand every detail."

She toyed with the stem of her glass.

"Now start by explaining you why you ran. Continue with the reason you cut off all communication." He sat back.

The tightness in his voice was the only evidence of his wrath. She'd been wrong to think there was anything benign in his discussion. But she was surprised that she hadn't seen it earlier. Obviously he was on guard. When they'd been together, he'd never disguised his emotions. He'd expressed his love, his rare displeasure, as well as his attraction for her.

He steepled his hands and studied her with cold, cold blue eyes. It was in that moment that she saw the full effect of the damage she'd caused.

A waiter brought salads, checked to see if they needed anything else then left them in solitude.

"Did you make sure no one was seated near us?" she asked, realizing that some potted palms had been placed between them and the rest of the diners.

"I thought I'd save you the embarrassment of having anyone watch me shackle you to the chair if you started to prevaricate."

She gasped.

"Said for effect only," he assured her. "I probably won't tie you up unless you beg me to."

Sarah picked up her salad fork.

With a wicked grin, he added, "Upending you over the table and blazing your ass isn't out of the question, though."

She dropped the fork, and it clattered onto the side of the plate.

"To make that easier, please remove your underwear."

"Uhm…"

"Now."

He lazed back with his wine. His salad sat in front of him, ignored.

"I'm not sure what's going on here."

"You wanted to talk, but you also need to be dominated."

"I'm not certain about that, Reece."

"Honey, the fact that you sought me out proves that. You didn't seek me out at the bar. You and Julien colluded to set up an elaborate scene. Getting the St Andrew's cross and my duffel bag took some doing. Now take off your panties or I'll remove them for you."

A little shocked, she sat there.

Motions calm and controlled, he set down the glass, pushed back his chair and stood.

Her mouth dried as she looked up at him.

He offered his hand. As if hypnotized, she tossed her napkin next to her plate, then placed her palm against his. An electrical spark shot up her forearm. With inexorable force, he pulled her up.

"Put your hands on the table," he instructed when she was only inches from him.

Damn. The man terrified her as much as he intrigued her. Hadn't that always been the conundrum for her? Until that last day, when she'd run, desire had outweighed the fear.

After releasing her, he took a step back and nodded toward the table.

Her heartbeat increasing exponentially, she got into position.

As if they were the only two people on the small island, he lifted her dress.

"Your underwear…what do you call them?"

"Boy shorts," she supplied, mortified that they were in a restaurant with her dress around her waist.

"They're different from what you usually wear. I like them. They show your ass cheeks nicely."

Without warning, he slipped the material down. The breeze whispered across her bare skin.

"Better," he said.

She stepped out of the panties, and he scooped them up from the concrete floor.

"Stay there," he told her.

"Now I'm nervous."

"Good."

She glanced over her shoulder at him, in time to see him shove her underwear in his pants pocket.

"Face forward, Sarah."

Reacting instead of thinking, she did as he said.

He caressed both of her buttocks. His hands were strong, competent, and she was becoming molten. His sensual competence was beyond compare.

"Reece, are you—?" Breath whooshed from her when he slapped her right cheek, hard.

He turned and hit her on the other cheek.

"Damn," she said softly.

"You may be seated." He lowered her dress back into place.

"I didn't expect that."

"All along, I was probably too lax with you."

"Not at all," she protested.

"What I did didn't work."

"It was about me," she said, pushing her salad plate to the side. "Not you. Even though you said you wouldn't accept my apology, I'm sorry, regardless. Leaving you that way was thoughtless."

"Heartless," he corrected.

She winced.

"You could have accepted my calls, returned an email, even left a note."

She looked back at him. "I was scared."

"We made an agreement. Remember?"

"I do."

"Tell me."

After everything they'd shared—then and just today—this should have been easier. She used to beg him to flog her and fuck her. "We went to the symphony," she said. "Before you tied me up for the first time, we sat down across the table from each other." Much as they were tonight. "You told me that we had to talk before anything happened that might frighten me." She exhaled and took a shaky drink. "You promised you'd never do anything to me, with me, without discussing it first."

"Did I keep my word?"

The wine sloshed over the rim as she pushed the glass away. "Yes."

"Every time?"

"Yes."

"Was there anything that scared you, ever?"

"What is this, a cross-examination?" She fought to suppress her sudden anger and frustration.

"Answer the question, Sarah. You wanted to talk. Talk."

"You know I was scared, more than once."

"And what did we do?"

"We stopped. You'd hold me or have me put on some clothes. Sometimes we left the bedroom and went into the living room because you thought that would totally change my mindset."

"In the two years we spent together, did I ever give you reason to believe I was unworthy of your trust?"

For long moments, she didn't answer. She closed her eyes to gather strength. "No."

"So what changed?"

"I found a collar in your dresser drawer."

"Ah. That was meant to be a surprise."

55

"It was. Believe me."

He shook his head. "And?" he prompted.

"And?" She leaned toward him. "Is that all you can say?"

"I'm confused, Sarah. You found a gift I bought for you. What else do you want me to say?"

"Reece." How could he be so clueless? "I found a steel, silver-colored collar in a red velvet pouch. In your dresser drawer."

"I heard you the first time."

"Was it for me?"

"Of course it was for you. Did you think it was for someone else? Did you think I'd ask someone else to wear it? That it meant something casual?"

"No." She felt as if they were having two separate conversations, with neither of them comprehending the other's point of view. "Do you really not understand what the problem was?"

"No," he said. "I don't."

Emotion, angst and upset coiled in her. "You wanted to put that thing on me?"

"You are correct. I was waiting for the right time for us to discuss it."

"That's what you don't understand. For me, the time would never have been right."

"Sarah, for Christ's sake, I loved you. I wanted to marry you. And you're telling me you ran away, vanished, because you found a collar in my dresser drawer?"

She remembered the moment, the horror. She'd been crazy in love with him, and she'd had a suspicion that he'd been planning to propose. They'd had discussions about the future, even about rings. "That…thing wasn't a nice piece of jewelry that I could have passed off as a necklace."

"Of course not. It wasn't meant that way."

"The whole world would have known."

"Is that your issue? You didn't want others to know you were mine. How's that different from a wedding ring?"

"Were you always so obtuse?" she asked.

"Were you always so ridiculous?" he countered.

"This is why I didn't stay to talk," she said. "There are certain things you can't be reasonable about. You wouldn't have been happy until I gave in and let you snap it into place."

"And thrown away the key."

Her pulse stuttered.

"Damn it, Sarah. Really? Do you think I would have done that?"

"Yes."

"I never made you do anything you didn't want to, until you were ready. We could have worked it out."

"That's my point." She curled her hands into tight fists. "You'd have been relentless. You would have worn down my defenses. I'd have capitulated to make you happy. And that wouldn't have worked for me. I would have ended up resenting you. I know what it represents to you."

"Tell me."

Part of her thought this discussion was ludicrous. But, as she'd told Julien, she hadn't really expected Reece to make it easy for her. "Ownership."

"Like a car?"

"No." She reached for a sip of wine. The conversation seemed surreal. "Like a slave."

"And that would have changed our relationship, how?"

"I wasn't a slave. I could never have been a slave."

"A *slave*. That's your word, Sarah. It's not mine. It was never mine."

She scowled, mentally sifting back through their numerous conversations about submission and Dominance.

"At any rate, tell me what you think that would have meant to you."

She took a breath. "I would have been at your mercy all the time."

"Go on."

"It would have meant that I put your needs above mine. That I subjugated my will to yours." She picked at the edge of her napkin.

He closed his hand over hers. "Look at me when you talk to me," he said.

She was spared from further discussion when the waiter returned to collect the salad plates.

Seeing the untouched food, he asked, "Is everything okay?"

"Fine," Reece said. "Hold off on the main course for about twenty minutes."

The man nodded then left them alone. She was aware of a little more noise around them as, apparently, more diners were being seated on the other part of the patio.

Without her really noticing, the sun had set, and solar lights spilled out a gentle, soothing blue beam that didn't defuse the tension between them.

"I'm waiting," Reece prompted.

Tension arced between them.

"My whole life would have been wrapped up in thinking about you, trying to please you. And what about me? I wasn't as strong as I am now. You would have consumed me, Reece."

"Well then, in that case, you were right to run."

Sarah frowned. She'd expected him to deny it or argue, but to essentially agree with her? "Do you deny it?"

"We can't go back in time. But tell me, what is a collar?"

"What is *this*?" she countered. "A pseudo-intellectual discussion?"

"Humor me," he suggested, still holding her hand. "Let's keep it at this level, rather than a personal one, for now."

"We had friends in the lifestyle, Reece. We both know what it means."

"I know what it means to me. Educate me about *you*."

When he used a tone that sounded engaged and interested, she was helpless. "The collar...it was unyielding." She shivered.

"Of course it was. That's the point."

"It had an O-ring on it. So you could use it for bondage, as well?"

"It was more decorative, but yes. Your point is well taken."

"God."

"Keep talking. Beyond that, what does it mean?"

"It's a symbol. An expression to the whole world that you've claimed me."

"Only people in the lifestyle would recognize its significance."

"Reece, if I wore a collar that obvious, everyone would know something was up."

Repeatedly, he feathered his thumb across the back of her hand. "So your objection is that others would know you're my sexual plaything?"

"No. Yes."

"Why would that bother you? Most couples have sex."

"Why wouldn't it bother you?"

"Because I was proud of you. Because our rings would have shown our commitment to each other."

His comment caught her off guard. "You would have worn a wedding ring?"

"Proudly."

"I'd have bet you would have refused." What else had she presumed? What else had she gotten wrong?

"The collar would never have meant that you were my sexual plaything. I find that insulting. It would have demonstrated your devotion to me."

She pulled her hand back.

"There's nothing nefarious about it. I never intended to put you on a leash and tether you to a wall while I was gone. Nor did I consider buying you a steel cage."

That image made her recoil, just as she was sure he had intended.

"To me, Sarah, your love was my most treasured possession."

Tears stung her eyes.

"I valued you above all others. I spent a week shopping for a collar. When I couldn't find something that suited, I had it made." More quietly, he continued. "Maybe I was wrong about you. Perhaps you didn't possess the sense of self to wear my collar without losing yourself. But frankly I was never worried about that. I would have never been interested in a woman without a backbone. A woman who considered herself less than my equal wouldn't have kept my interest. And I certainly would never have considered dating her, let alone marrying her. But perhaps you knew yourself better than I thought I knew you."

Not much left her speechless, but this—he—did.

"I would have never put it on you, let alone locked it into place and thrown away the key without a lot of discussion with you. Treating you with great care was of paramount importance."

"And what if I had refused it?"

"I would have naturally hoped you would reconsider. I would have asked repeatedly, hoping to wear you down. But I would have never forced you into it."

She suddenly couldn't breathe.

Instead of wine, she grabbed her water and took a big gulp as she struggled to right her skewed emotions.

The waiter returned with their dinner plates.

"Spiny lobster?" she asked. Her mouth watered despite

the conversation that had stolen her appetite and fractured everything she'd taken for granted.

The waiter nodded his confirmation. "Melted butter," he said, indicating a silver-colored cup. "And blue cheese butter. Anything else I can bring you?"

After ensuring she had everything she needed, Reece said, "This is perfect. Thank you."

"Yes, sir. Enjoy your meal."

Despite her nerves and upset, her stomach grumbled. "You remembered that I said I wanted to try this?" she asked when they were alone.

"Sarah, I remember every word you ever uttered."

She speared a piece of the meat and dipped it in the blue cheese butter. The combination, succulent lobster with clarified butter and pungent cheese, was an explosion on her taste buds. She closed her eyes.

"I always enjoyed watching you eat," he said. "You could make a saint dream of going to hell."

She looked at him. His gaze was locked on her, and she realized that he hadn't taken a bite.

His single-minded focus and pursuit were something else she'd missed when she was with other men.

"So how is it?"

"Everything I imagined. Not as sweet as Maine lobster. And, this might sound strange, but it tastes a bit meatier. I'm a fan." She took a sip of wine. "Even this was well thought out."

"I asked the sommelier. She tells me the Sauvignon Blanc is not intimidated by the melted butter."

"Seriously?"

"Could I make that up?"

"I suppose not." She grinned for the first time that evening.

He smiled back. For a moment, just a flicker of time, she

was reminded of the easy evenings they'd once shared at home.

"Everything is perfect."

"You might think I was trying to seduce you," he said.

She regarded him over the rim of the glass. "Are you?"

"Depends."

"On?"

"How brave you are. How honest you're willing to be."

"I'm not sure I understand."

"Tell me what you really want. You accepted my dinner invitation."

"Invitation?"

"You could have refused. Why did you come? Curiosity, or something more? Julien suggested that you were hoping to exorcise my hold over you. Earlier, our scene... Did it work?"

She remained silent, and she pretended that her hand didn't waver as she put the glass down. "No," she said finally. "I was left more restless. And, to be honest, this dinner is making it worse."

"How so?"

"The way you put your attention on me... It's as if I'm the only woman in the world."

"To me, you always have been."

Her lungs deflated. "I hurt you."

"Devastated."

She swallowed deeply. "Julien said as much. I told him that was an exaggeration."

"No."

"I'm not sure what to say."

"I will tell you this much, Sarah. I don't make the same mistake twice."

From what she'd seen in the press about his recent success, she'd have said he never made mistakes.

"If you want me to beat you and fuck you, I will. But there will be rules around it. No promises, no expectations. We'll both call it what it is, exorcising the demon of the past. After the weekend, you go home, we never see each other again."

With boldness that surprised her, scared her, she asked, "And if I want more?"

"Right now, that's not an option. You'd have to earn my trust, show me you deserved it. If I scared you before, I would terrify you now. Before I'd consider anything with you, Sarah, I would test you in ways you couldn't imagine."

"Are you trying to scare me?"

"Is it working?"

"A little," she admitted.

"Good. You should be frightened. The collar would only be the beginning of what I would demand from you. I wouldn't be satisfied with anything less than your total honesty. I would want to own every one of your reactions. Even that wouldn't be enough. I'd want to know your every thought, every fear, every inhibition. I'd want to hear every scream and savor every tear. And I'd demand you turn to me to wipe them. There would be no place for you to hide."

The chill in his voice rippled through her.

"Well, what will it be, Sarah? Shall I just walk you back to your room after dinner?" He raised an eyebrow. "How brave are you now?"

CHAPTER THREE

Reece watched several emotions chase across her face. Her lips had parted as she'd listened to him. Now, slowly, she closed her mouth. Then she frowned. He saw shock. Disbelief. Resignation. And now, with the set of her lips, determination.

Reece told himself that her answer didn't matter. She'd vanished once, and he'd survived it. When he'd accepted the invitation to Julien's party, Reece had expected to find some female companionship for the weekend. Playing with her could be an interesting diversion, as long as he didn't allow himself to fall under her spell again.

"I'm sure that you're right that I should be scared. But maybe I'm more foolish than frightened. For right now, I'll settle for what you're offering."

"The weekend?"

She nodded.

He reached for the bottle of wine and topped off her glass. "Eat up. Your dinner is getting cold."

She picked up her fork, and he did the same.

"This really is good," she said.

He took a bite. "Agreed." He wasn't talking about the food.

In silence, they ate for a few minutes.

"I like it best with the blue cheese butter," she said.

"I prefer it with a squeeze of lemon."

She took one more bite then pushed her plate aside. The waiter appeared a few minutes later.

"Key lime pie for dessert?" he asked.

Sarah shook her head.

"Coffee?" Reece offered.

"I'm done."

"Bill it to my room, please," he told the waiter.

"Certainly, sir."

As soon as they were alone, he stood and pulled back her chair.

Taking her hand, he said, "Come with me."

"Not upstairs?"

"Not yet."

He led her down a path toward the ocean.

"Moonlight stroll?"

"Among other things."

In the dimness, he saw her eyebrows draw together.

The resort had done an artful job with using shrubbery to make the path clear. There was enough lighting to be safe, but not enough to ruin the Caribbean ambiance.

Only one other couple was on the private beach, and he guided her away from them.

The resort loomed in the distance, providing a point of reference. Clouds drifted in front of the moon, casting shadows before moving on.

He led her close to the ocean, where the sand was damp, packed, easier to walk on.

"Now what?" she asked when he pulled her to a stop.

"Naked."

"I beg your pardon?"

"I want you naked."

"Here?"

He waited.

She glanced around. Then she worried her lower lip. "You're serious?"

"If I help you undress, there will be a penalty."

"Will I like it?"

He remembered her teasing him like that in the past. Sometimes she'd opt to pay the price. Other times, she just wanted to know what her options were. When he spoke more harshly, she obeyed, even if it was slowly, reluctantly. "Do you like that dress?"

"I'll take that as a no," she said.

She kicked off her sandals. Then she pulled her dress over her head.

He took it from her, then said, "The bra, too."

"I was afraid of that."

He stood there while she removed it. "I may keep you like that for the whole weekend."

She opened her mouth but closed it without saying anything.

"Into the ocean."

"You remembered."

"I told you earlier," he said. "I remember every single word you say to me." He took off his jacket and spread it on the sand while she waded into the water, then he placed her dress and bra on top.

"Come on!" she called.

Reece stripped, dropping his clothes on top of hers.

She was already waist deep when he headed toward her.

When he was close, she splashed him. "Are you a strong swimmer?" he asked, dragging his hair back from his forehead.

"Awful," she insisted, slowly backing away.

"That's unfortunate." He stalked her.

She laughed, moving backwards. "No. Really. I'm a terrible swimmer."

Concentrating on her, he didn't reply.

"Reece?" She crossed her arms in front of her.

He dove beneath the water and came up behind her. After catching her up in his arms, he turned, then tossed her into the water.

Seconds later, she came up sputtering.

"You're wet, Sarah."

She wiped her hair back from her face. Then, shocking him, she dove beneath the water and swam strongly toward him. He momentarily lost sight of her, but then felt something against the back of his legs.

He pitched forward as his knees buckled.

"Don't underestimate the power of revenge," she told him when he regained his footing.

She'd used the distraction to move quite a bit closer to shore and, like a siren, stood there, feathering back the long strands of her hair from her eyes and wearing a brilliant smile.

"Come here," he said.

"I…"

He pointed to an imaginary spot directly in front of him. "Now."

With an exaggerated sway of her hips, she complied. "What can I do for you, Sir?" she asked, finger-combing her hair as she looked up at him.

Her nipples were tight beads, and goosebumps dotted her arms. She'd never been lovelier.

His cock hardened.

In the two years they'd been apart, he'd dated a handful of women, even played with a couple of subs at an exclusive club in the Colorado Rockies. But his body responded to her in a way it didn't with any other woman.

He reminded himself to be careful with this one. Despite the emotional damage she'd caused, he wanted her. Bad. No one had turned him on like she did. No one else had made him think of the future.

"What are you thinking?"

"About your breasts."

Salt water ran down her chest. "Do men ever think about anything else?"

"What's the question?"

She cupped her hand and scooped up water to toss at him.

He captured her wrist and dragged her closer.

"You're every bit as sexy as you ever were," she said, running her free hand down his upper arm.

Until he'd met her, he'd sworn off love. In fact, back in college, he, Julien, Kennedy and Grant had gotten drunk on a very expensive, and very stolen, bottle of Scotch as he lamented the fact that Mindy Bates had broken his heart.

He'd caught her in bed with one of their professors, and the lucky guy had been getting a blow job. Julien had started planning a strategy to get the guy fired. A remote video camera would be involved, along with sending the feed to the college's president.

Grant had clapped Reece on the back in sympathy.

But it was Kennedy who had been the real hero. His girl-friend, the amazing and sultry Samara, had flashed her gorgeous, enhanced breasts at the liquor store clerk while Kennedy had swiped the bottle from the shelf.

Then she'd been understanding while Kennedy had gone out with the guys. Reece had always thought that Kennedy should have married the woman. His family would have never agreed to that. Going to school in Texas had been as big a rebellion as he'd been allowed. The fact that Kennedy had finally relented and accepted family money and been packed off to an Ivy League graduate program had meant he had finally understood the weight of the mantle that would be transferred onto him when his father passed.

"What are you thinking?" Sarah asked.

"That you lied. About being a terrible swimmer."

"Yes, I did," she said.

Her triumphant grin made her eyes light up. The deadly combination forced him to hide a smile.

"The question is, what are you going to do about it, Mr McRae? Tie me up? Blindfold me?" Her words were breathless, laced with anticipation.

"Paddle your behind."

"When?" She moved her hand lower until she captured his balls.

"You never used to be so bold."

"Do you like it?"

"I'll get back to you on that."

She stroked his cock. "In a few minutes?"

He'd already been aroused. Now he was impossibly hard. "Five. Ten at the most."

She smiled, and he was reminded of the past. They'd shared a lot of teasing moments, both at the office then at home after he'd convinced her to move in. Even when she was starting her own business and she was working sixteen hour days, they'd taken time to talk on the phone, or he'd bring her takeout food.

Sarah leaned against him and put her forehead on his shoulder.

He resisted the impulse to wrap an arm around her and hold her close. They had the rest of the weekend. Nothing more.

She continued her rhythmic motion, and he stopped her.

"I'd like to save that for later," he said.

"Only if I can suck it."

Fuck. Yeah. The woman had definitely grown bolder in the last two years. Sarah Lovett had become a sex kitten. Would he survive it? The image of her on her knees, intent on his pleasure, made him throb. "That can be arranged. Let's go."

He released his hold on her. The brat stroked his cock another couple of times. "Be careful of disobeying me," he warned.

"Of course, Sir."

Sarah had chosen the right response, but the lightness in her tone had robbed the words of their genuineness.

"I'm warning you."

"I heard you, Sir," she reassured him.

He followed her from the sea and, on shore, picked up her dress and helped her into it, not an easy feat with her body being wet.

"I seem to be having difficulty keeping my clothes on around you."

He tucked her bra into his jacket pocket.

"Am I going to get my lingerie back?"

"I wouldn't count on it," he replied. He shook the sand from his jacket then draped it around her shoulders.

"Thank you."

Reece liked to look at her, but suddenly he didn't want other men ogling her. After shucking water from his legs, he pulled on his trousers.

"You were commando?" she asked. "In those pants?"

"I'm not a fan of underwear for either of us," he replied.

"I'm sorry I didn't notice."

The way his cock was still responding made him glad that she hadn't noticed.

As he'd finished dressing, she scooped up her sandals and carried them by the straps.

When they neared the resort, he said, "Wait a minute." He picked a bright pink bloom and tucked it behind her ear, into her damp hair.

"Hibiscus," she said. "One of my favorites."

"Lucky guess." He didn't know a dandelion from a daffodil and didn't much care to learn. That was why florists existed.

"Thank you. For that, as well as the swim," she said.

"Wondering what other surprises you have in store for me," he replied.

They stopped again so she could rinse off her feet at the outdoor shower, and he offered an arm for support as she slipped her shoes back on.

Inside the resort, the lobby was loud and bustling. Air-conditioning blasted them, chilling his still-damp skin. Bottles of champagne were being passed around, sans glasses. In an alcove, a string quartet appeared to be playing. Since he couldn't hear anything over all of Julien's friends and acquaintances, it was difficult to say. "Need anything before we head up?"

"McRae!"

Recognizing the voice above the droning noise, he held up his hand to signal Sarah to stop.

"Someone you know?" she asked.

"College buddy. Went to school together until his mommy and daddy shipped him off to Massachusetts and away from our questionable friendship and morals. As you see, questionable morals trump family expectations."

"Is that Kennedy Aldrich?" She looked at one of his oldest friends then back to him. "Wait. You know Kennedy Aldrich?"

"Have I finally impressed you?"

72

"In a big way. First Julien, then Kennedy Aldrich?"

"I'm only impressing you because of my friends?"

"We're talking about Kennedy Aldrich, Reece," she said, as if that explained everything.

"He's a normal guy." Could drink with the best of them, cheat on a test or two, drive too fast, don a disguise to dodge the paparazzi, wield a whip, complete a deal on the golf course and still go on a morning talk show.

"Who's this?" Kennedy asked by way of greeting.

"Nice to see you, too, Aldrich," Reece said.

The way Kennedy ignored him and honed in on Sarah pissed Reece off, just a little.

She extended her hand, returning the man's smile. "Sarah Lovett."

"Sarah Lovett? *The* Sarah Lovett?" Friendly expression gone, Kennedy looked at Reece. "Do we need a bottle of Scotch?"

"Did I miss something?" she asked.

Kennedy took her hand. "Man went through a fortune of my best stuff when you vanished, Ms Lovett."

"Does everyone know?" she asked Reece. Her tone held a combination of apology and horror.

"That you ran away and broke his heart? Only the people he gets drunk with," Kennedy assured her. "I'm surprised and delighted to meet you."

"Wanting the floor to open up and swallow me," she said.

"You can let go of her hand now," Reece told Kennedy.

Slowly he did so.

"I'll, er, wait in my room for you?" she suggested.

"Mine," Reece responded. He reached into his pocket, moved aside her panties and pulled out his key. "Room nine thirty-seven."

She nodded.

"Be waiting on your knees. Naked."

Though she flushed, she responded with, "Of course. Sir."

"Very nice," Kennedy said. "You've had some training."

"From Reece," she said. After excusing herself, she walked toward the bank of elevators, and he watched her until the doors slid closed behind her.

"What the hell are you doing with her? Are you a slow learner?" Kennedy asked. "You didn't seek her out, did you?"

"No chance."

"Since no one gets in without an invitation, I'm assuming Julien aided and abetted her? I thought he promised to keep her away from you."

"She convinced him. I imagine he had a hard time telling her no."

"Not sure I could have, either. You told us she was beautiful. At the time, I was sure it was the delusion of heartbreak speaking."

It wasn't. And time had only made her more attractive in Reece's eyes. "I'm not sure whether to thank him or throw the first punch."

"I brought a case of Scotch to the island as a birthday present for the old man. But if you want a couple of bottles from it, I'd say you deserve them."

"May take you up on it."

"Tell you what. I'll send up some. Trying to convince you to buy stock in the company, anyway."

"Do you always have an ulterior motive?"

"It's my God-given obligation to increase the Aldrich bottom line for the next generation. Failure will not be treated kindly."

"Said without much hostility."

"It's still there. Just more cleverly disguised than in the past," Kennedy replied.

"You here with anyone?"

"No. Avoiding young ladies of Mayflower lineage has

become a full-time job. Who the hell knew there'd be that many of them?"

Kennedy was photographed with someone new at almost every event. Recently he'd been named Bachelor of the Year by a popular gossip magazine, and a handful of women had competed for the honor of removing his name from future consideration. Reece knew his friend was under tremendous pressure from his family to carry on the Aldrich lineage, but he'd shown little desire to find a baby mama.

"I take it you're not sharing your Sarah?"

"I'm not."

"Pity. Not that I blame you. She's a beautiful woman."

In his pocket, Reece ran his thumb across her lacy boy shorts. "She was a coward."

"There's a fine line between real fear and being a coward," Kennedy replied. "I've walked it myself a few times."

Reece nodded.

"Enjoy your evening. I'll see what delights our host has provided." Kennedy glanced toward a group of seated and apparently single ladies. "And hope none of them are angling for a three-karat rock from my grandmother's safe."

"I'm meeting Julien for basketball in the morning."

"I may crash your party unless I find a reason to stay in bed."

"I'm not sure whether to hope I see you or not." Reece excused himself to catch an elevator.

Kennedy's words played in Reece's mind. Kennedy had more experience with subs and had seen more examples of the complex relationship dynamics than Reece ever would. Had he unfairly labeled Sarah as a coward? And would that make any difference? She'd run from him without a word. He'd lain in bed night after night trying to figure out why she'd left. Another man? Maybe she'd found someone else. Or fallen out of love. In his wildest thoughts, he'd

SIERRA CARTWRIGHT

wondered if something from her past had caught up with her.

At first he'd walked around in numb disbelief. Then he'd been hurt. Days later, anger had set in. Eventually fear had replaced it. He'd woken up in a sweat, wondering if she was out there, cold, afraid, hurting, needing him.

In the dozens of scenarios he'd dreamt up to explain her absence, the fucking collar hadn't been one of them.

Even now, her reaction seemed absurd.

How could she ever have thought that she was anything less than the most important thing in his life? That he'd compel her to wear something she abhorred? And, worse, why the hell hadn't she trusted him enough to turn to him?

He might have thought that he'd dealt with all the emotions she'd caused when she'd gone away, but there they were, rippling in the present, threatening the future.

The bell dinged and the doors slid open. He walked down the hall and noticed that his door was propped open by the security latch.

When he entered, Sarah was on her knees, facing him, naked. Nothing mattered except Sarah and the moment.

She'd draped her dress across the foot of his bed and had carefully tucked her shoes beneath the mattress. Her fingers were laced behind her neck. The image of her there, breasts invitingly thrust toward him, held him riveted.

"Before you left, I would somehow make it through the day because I imagined coming home to you."

"I'm here now."

He hung the 'do not disturb' sign and closed the door behind him before facing her. "I often wanted to find you like this, in that position. Who taught you?"

"You did."

"Two years ago, you weren't as graceful, as peaceful."

"I've been practicing. In the hopes that I'd have the chance

76

to show you what I've learnt. You kept asking me to do it. But I lacked the confidence. I took some yoga classes. Went to a couple of workshops at a club in Denver. After we broke up—"

"After you ran."

"After I ran," she repeated. "I found regular guys boring. I wanted what we'd had."

He rested his shoulders against the wall. "You had some success in your search?"

She shifted uncomfortably, more from the question than from the position, he guessed.

"No. Finding someone at the club who'd whip me wasn't difficult. And I went on a few dates. I met a few really nice guys who I found boring. And a few Neanderthals who were also boring."

"Worse than me?"

"Swinging from ropes and scratching their hairy bellies. Much worse than you." She smiled, but let it quickly fall. "I haven't had a serious relationship with anyone since you."

He didn't want her words to matter. But they did. "We need to shower," he said.

"I was afraid you'd never offer."

He extended his hand to help her up, and he continued pulling until she was against him. "I'm going to fuck you hard tonight," he warned.

"Good."

With that, she extracted herself from his grip and flounced toward the bathroom. In the doorway, she paused and looked over her shoulder. "For the record, I never found you boring." Then she crooked her finger, silently inviting him to follow her.

What the hell had he agreed to? "You're forgetting who the Dom is."

"Remind me."

She was already in the shower stall under the spray when he joined her. "I think you're looking for a beating," he said, pinning her arms above her head.

"We had discussions about being a brat," she said. "You were clear that you don't tolerate that kind of behavior. So, let me be honest since you only promised me a weekend. I want you."

He inserted a leg between hers.

"I masturbate to fantasies of you," she confessed.

"Do you?"

"I have dreams about you. And more, I want to please you."

"Hump my thigh. Get yourself off."

When they'd started dating, she'd been somewhat inexperienced. He'd found her naïveté charming. It had taken a while to break down some of her barriers, but a few inhibitions had remained, even at the end.

She adjusted her position, bending her knees. "This would be easier if you'd release my arms."

"Deal with it."

"Yes, Sir," she said, tilting her pelvis forward.

"Nice." He braced himself to take more of her weight. "Did I embarrass you in front of my friend?"

"No, Sir. I understood."

"What did you understand?"

"Earlier you said you'd test me. You were proving that you meant it."

"Is that all?"

She closed her eyes and sank her teeth into her lower lip.

"Answer the question, Sarah."

"No." She opened her eyes. "Submission is part of being with you. You expect it at all times, and you don't hide who you are or what we share from anyone."

He nodded. "Your pussy is getting slick."

"Yes," she whispered.

"Are you close to coming?"

"Yes."

"Don't."

She looked up, took a breath and nodded. "Anything you say, Sir."

He loosened his grip. "Wash me."

"My pleasure."

Reece knew she'd been close to coming, and that she'd stopped without hesitation or protest showed him how hard she was trying.

She unwrapped the hotel's bar of soap and lathered it before asking him, "Front or back first, Sir?"

The idea of her hands on his dick was problematic. He was trying to show who was in charge.

"If you'll turn around?" she asked.

He did, and she ran her hands over his shoulders before making swirling motions on her way down.

She crouched to rub his buttocks.

"I'm sure my ass isn't that salty," he said.

"Trying to be thorough, Sir."

With the same deliberate intention, she washed his legs. "You're still working out," she observed.

"It helps with the stress level."

"Do you mind facing me?"

When he did, his semi-hard cock was only inches from her face. Looking up at him, she licked the head.

"More," he instructed.

She took his length into her mouth, gagging as he hit the back of her throat.

He showed mercy, for a moment, then he captured her head and held it prisoner while she licked and sucked.

He closed his eyes. Her sweet moans drove him on.

It wouldn't take him long to come, he knew.

Damn vixen changed her pace, moving faster and faster. "Sarah."

"Uh-huh," she mumbled.

Flogging her had given him a hard-on. And he'd been in a state of semi-arousal since. He was contemplating stopping her when she tightened her grip. "*Fuck.*" He groaned as thick, hot cum pulsed from him.

He reached for the wall with one hand, needing it for balance, while he kept the other tangled in her hair.

His perfect little submissive—the woman he'd wanted as his own—captured every drop.

Then, shocking him, humbling him, she lapped up the last drop, looked up at him and swallowed.

"Sarah…"

"Thank you, Sir," she said.

Where had this woman been while they'd been living together?

He helped her to stand and gently kissed her forehead. "Thank *you*," he said. "But if you think that means I'm done with you—"

"It always has in the past."

"You really are looking for trouble."

"Of the most delicious kind."

He backed her against the tile and again put his leg between hers. "Finish yourself off."

She rocked back and forth, fast then slow.

"Will you touch me, Sir?"

"I'll be a generous Dom and allow you sixty seconds to orgasm before denying you."

"But—"

"Be careful when you look for trouble with me, my Sarah."

"So, no paddling?"

"For that offense? Certainly not. Get on with it before I change my mind."

She pushed away from the tile and wrapped one arm around his neck. With her free hand, she made figure eights over her breasts, pinching her nipples as she did so.

"Creative," he acknowledged. "Thirty seconds left."

Her motions became frantic, and she made panting sounds as she rubbed up and down his leg.

"Reece…"

"Do it," he said. "Come on me, Sarah."

He pinched her ass cheek.

She pitched forward with a scream. Her climax warmed his skin, satisfying him.

He supported her body as her breathing slowly returned to normal.

"Uhm. I never knew that could feel so good."

"You're welcome. Now wash yourself."

"I was hoping you would do it for me."

"I'm going to watch."

He scooped the bar of soap from the floor of the shower and handed it to her. "Take your time," he told her.

Even though she'd given him head and she'd masturbated herself on his leg, she still looked down as if embarrassed. More and more, she intrigued him.

She made a lather, slid the soap onto a shelf then glided her hand across her chest and breasts. She spent long, driving-him-mad seconds rubbing her forefingers back and forth over her nipples. "They're sensitive from the clips earlier."

He brushed her hands aside. "So, does this hurt?" He squeezed hard enough for her to suck air between her teeth. "How about now?" He twisted each in an opposite direction.

"Damn, Sir."

"Harder?" He demonstrated. "Less pressure?" He eased off a little.

"Harder." She shook her head. "I mean, whatever you say."

"Good girl." He squeezed tight.

"Sir, you're making me horny again."

"Unfortunate that you have to wait a while before your next orgasm."

"Then a lighter touch would be appreciated."

He continued to torment her relentlessly.

She gasped. "Please, please, please…"

He wasn't sure what she was begging for. Reece was willing to bet she didn't know, either.

Instinctively she swayed toward him. Knowing he could make her come by just flicking a finger across her clit, he backed off. "You need to finish washing."

"Yes," she said.

Her eyes were glassy as she reached for the soap again. Water ran down her body in gentle rivulets, rinsing her clean as quickly as she lathered.

"Take your time," he reminded her.

"Do you have any dollar bills?" she teased.

"Earlier could have definitely qualified as a lap dance," he said.

As she soaped her mound, he wondered which of them was being tortured most.

"You remembered how I like your pubic hair," he said.

"I got a Brazilian wax."

"Good start."

She frowned up at him. "Sir?"

"I've decided I want the small strip removed."

She opened her mouth then closed it without saying anything else.

"You really are learning."

He waited patiently while she finished her front side. She

turned away, and he held up her hair while she did her shoulders.

"I'll help with your pussy," he said. He skipped the soap and used only his hand, sliding between her labia lips, easing back the hood of her clitoris. He cupped a handful of water and used it to rinse her, front and back. Then he eased the tip of his forefinger into her ass.

She tightened up and he withdrew.

"That will be part of our play," he told her.

"Now?" she asked. "In the shower?"

"Later."

"Part of testing me?"

"If you want to call it that. It pleases me."

"It freaks me out."

"Then we'll talk about it first. And you always have a safe word."

"Cream pie."

"You can't safe word more than twelve hours in advance," he said against her ear.

"I was afraid of that."

"Can't blame you for trying." He nipped her ear.

She went rigid for a second, then melted into him.

"This is how it was always supposed to have been," he said.

"Mostly, it was."

"Yeah." He remembered.

He inserted his finger up her rectum as far as the first knuckle. This time, she caught her breath, but she didn't protest.

"How's that?"

"Not as bad as the first time."

He washed his hands then turned off the faucet. "Wait there." He opened the glass door, stepped out and grabbed a towel. He returned with it and draped it around her.

"You always took good care of me."

"I always would have."

Her small smile froze then fractured.

He turned away and dried himself off.

"For the rest of the night," she said, "can we forget the past?"

"It defines who we are."

"I agree. So why not see how we interact now?"

He nodded and offered his hand. "Pretend it's an olive branch."

She accepted.

"Julien had my toy bag delivered."

"Oh?"

"Drop the towel and choose three different items." He pointed to the closet.

She retrieved the bag and put it on the bed. The only sounds in the room were the hum of the air conditioner, the husk of the bag's zipper and her soft sighs.

Sarah Lovett had definitely evolved. Whether they were going to talk about the past or not, there was no doubt that she was much more confident. He liked the changes, he had to admit. And a traitorous part of him wondered if she would have had the same realizations if she hadn't found her own way.

The first thing she selected was a wooden paddle. "That's brave." When he'd looked through the contents earlier, he'd seen a milder, leather one. "Surprising choice."

"I figured you wanted me to remember it."

She placed the hood alongside it.

Finally, she selected soft handcuffs.

"You can put those back. Nothing that prevents you from getting up and leaving."

Her head snapped back as if he'd smacked her. "Just for tonight," Sarah reminded him.

The hurt in her eyes would have convinced him, even if her words hadn't. "In that case, hand them to me."

He accepted the cuffs. After grabbing a length of nylon rope from the bag, he walked around to the far side of the bed. He lifted the box spring and looped the rope around the metal frame. Then he tied the rope to the cuffs.

"Great improvisation, Sir."

"Lie on your stomach. Reach across the mattress. But keep your feet flat on the floor."

He made a couple of adjustments as he secured her wrists. "Pull on them," he said.

She tested the restraints.

"Perfect," he said. He took a step back and looked at her. "You look beautiful, Sarah."

She squirmed.

"Say thank you."

"Thank you, Sir," she repeated.

"Spread your legs farther apart."

"That's a bit terrifying," she said, but she complied.

"Not to worry. I won't hit your pussy with the paddle."

She pulled on the restraints. "Was that meant to be comforting or reassuring?"

"Not at all."

"Well, it wasn't," she said.

"Turn your toes inward."

"Sir?"

He nudged her feet, and she understood what he meant. The position left her a bit more vulnerable. "I love the way you look. Your butt thrust up, the gorgeous view of your pussy." He fingered her, teasing until he felt her grow moist. Then she began to move. "Keep still. I'm not going to get you off."

"Ah... What if I can't help it?"

"You can. Focus on anything but my touch." He inserted a finger inside her.

"I don't think you know what you're asking from me, Sir."

"I do. You're beyond the easy stuff. Think about pleasing me." He pressed a finger against her G-spot, and she rose onto the balls of her feet. "Stay in position like a good girl." He placed the palm of his free hand on the small of her back and forced her back down.

She made soft, mewling sounds. Despite his command, she was unable to stay still. He relented, withdrawing his finger.

"Sir!"

At one time, he'd known her body well. But now she was even more responsive. How was it possible to want her more now than he had two years ago?

He moved away from her. She swayed her hips then let her body sink deeper into the mattress.

"You had an orgasm in the shower, and, if I'm not mistaken, you gave yourself one before dinner."

She mumbled something he couldn't make out.

"Repeat that?"

When she didn't respond, he asked a second time.

"I'm not sure if I should."

Intrigued, he said, "I insist."

"I'm acting like the greedy sub you accuse me of being. I want you to give me an orgasm, Sir."

"In good time," he promised.

"And I want it now."

"You'll get it when I choose, delicious sub," he said.

"I was afraid of that."

"It will be more powerful if you wait."

"I was afraid you'd say that, too."

He walked around to the far side of the bed and squatted in front of her. "Breathe," he instructed.

She lifted her head a bit. "Do you know how difficult that is when all I can see is your cock?"

With a grin, he stroked her hair. Then he stood.

"Oh, good. Now it's only an inch from my mouth."

"Waiting is good for the soul."

"So you keep saying." She dropped her head back onto the mattress.

"How are the bonds? Circulation?"

"I'm fine. Honestly."

As if she'd said them, he heard her unspoken words. *Get on with it.* "At my leisure, Sarah."

She didn't respond.

Reece ran his fingers over her shoulders and down her arms, checking her muscles. Ascertaining that she really was all right, he went back to the other side of the bed. "Keep your head down," he said.

"I think you've got a diabolical streak."

"Or two."

He picked up the hood and returned to her. As gently as possible, he dug his fingers in her hair and lifted her head so that he could look into her eyes, giving her nowhere to hide. "I know this was always a struggle for you, but you added it to the bag, and you chose it."

"This is part of that diabolical streak, isn't it?"

"Yes, ma'am," he said. "It is."

Her smile touched a place inside him that he had thought long dead.

"You can safe word, and I won't hold it against you."

"Put it on me, Sir."

He nodded and released his grip. "Turn your head to the side so I can figure out how to do this without getting your hair all over the place."

It took a couple of adjustments, but he finally managed to situate it properly. "How's that?"

"Hot. Not like in sexy."

"It's hot like in sexy, as well," he said. And it was. Her trust was the ultimate aphrodisiac. "You can breathe okay?"

"Yes."

"If you're uncomfortable in any way or need a rest, use the word yellow." He walked around, looking at her from every angle.

Obviously aware of his scrutiny, she shifted.

"I want to watch you for a minute."

"Yes, Sir."

Her words were softened by the mask.

In silence, he continued to regard her. At one time, she would have fidgeted, said something humorous or made some noises. But she kept still.

"You've got a small welt," he said, "here." He took a step toward her and traced a faint mark on her skin. He was Dom enough to enjoy the sight left by his flogger.

"I saw it earlier," she said. "I was hoping for others to match it."

"If anything, the paddle will leave a bruise."

"I'm not picky, Sir." After thirty seconds, she exhaled deeply, and her body went slack.

"Very nice."

"Thank you, Sir."

Because the bed was king-sized, her body was on perfect display. Her sun-kissed hair pooled around her shoulders. Her ass was upturned, waiting. She was managing to keep her toes in place, pointing toward each other.

He picked up the paddle and pressed it against her buttocks.

"Yes," she whispered.

"What was the transgression, sub?"

"I lied about not being a strong swimmer."

"And you did so wilfully."

"Gleefully," she said.

He grinned. There'd been a reason he'd missed her so badly. Her honesty, her sassiness.

"So how many do you deserve?"

"Three should be sufficient for me to learn my lesson."

"Three?" he echoed.

"Okay, fine. Five, Sir. Ten from that thing would kill me."

"Ten it is," he said, knowing full well that was what she wanted.

He laid the paddle lengthwise down her spine so that she would be aware of its heft.

Then he vigorously rubbed her upper thighs and buttocks. She struggled to stay in position, and her tiny sounds made him anxious to get on with claiming her. "Ready?"

"Probably not," she admitted.

He picked up the paddle and gave it a couple of practice swings. To prepare her, to scare her, he hit the mattress.

She yelped.

"I didn't touch you."

"Mean, Sir."

He grinned. "How many did we agree on?"

"Ten, S—"

Before she'd finished speaking, he caught her beneath the buttock and lifted her onto her toes.

"Wow."

Since he'd landed the wood precisely, blazing both thighs, she remained in position. "Wow?"

"Ouch. But a good ouch."

This time, he hit her right buttock. She reacted by moving left, so he immediately placed the third on her other cheek. "Return to neutral," he told her.

After a deep breath, she followed his instruction.

Her skin blazed red from his punishment. Even though

he'd recently ejaculated, he was becoming aroused. "Where would you like the next one?"

It took her a moment to respond, as if she were considering her answer. "Wherever you say."

"Tell me what you want."

"Beneath my buttocks, Sir."

She tensed in expectation, so he paddled her right in the middle of her curvy ass.

"Sir!"

Immediately he spanked her where she'd requested.

"Thank you." Her body went limp.

"Halfway there," he told her. "Do you need to rest or use your safe word?"

"No, Sir."

The first time he'd spanked her, she'd taken four or five breaks. This courage and commitment astounded him.

He ran a finger between her legs. She responded by wriggling toward him. His lightest touch made her wet. The musky scent of her arousal hung on the air.

Again, he whacked the mattress. While she whimpered, he gave her another uppercut, directly above the previous one.

A light sheen of dew appeared on her skin. Crimson lines marred her behind.

He delivered his seventh stroke below the fifth. He finished her off, alternating between high and low until her entire butt blazed from his wooden paddle.

She was panting and thrashing by the time he was done.

"I'm going to fuck you."

"Please."

He tossed aside the paddle and grabbed a condom from the toy bag. According to the package, it was ultra-thin, for her pleasure. His, too. "I'm going to put a pillow beneath your stomach."

As much as she could, she moved to help him.

The sight of her, pussy moist and ready for him, skin dewy, wrists secured by his cuffs, hair in passionate disarray and head obscured by the hood, made his cock throb. He pressed a thumb against her clit.

She groaned. "You know what you're doing, don't you, Sir?"

He positioned his cockhead at her entrance.

"Please don't make me wait any longer."

Holding her waist, he pulled her back as he thrust inside her.

She expelled a deep breath.

Her fit was familiar, perfect.

"Fuck me. Fuck me, fuck me, *fuck me*," she begged, wriggling backwards to meet him.

"Do that some more."

It couldn't have been easy with the way he held her, the restraints and the angle of her feet, but she moved her hips, seeking him out, urging him deeper.

He bent his knees for leverage then surged up.

She cried out.

Her sounds drove him on. He thrust hard, giving her everything he had, imprisoning her, claiming her. "Come for me, Sarah."

"Thank you."

Her foot slipped as she sought purchase. He worked one arm between her and the pillow to give her extra support. Then he moistened a finger and worked it into her ass.

She hissed.

"That's it. Give me your orgasm. Give it to me." He fucked her pussy and moved his finger.

"Overwhelming."

"Give it to me," he demanded.

She bucked against him.

He moved his forearm slightly to change the angle of her hips. Her internal muscles clenched, milking his cock. His balls drew up in response. Holding back his orgasm while he concentrated on hers became a struggle.

"Now, Sarah. *Now.*"

With a scream, she shuddered and thrashed before going limp. But he wasn't done with her. He changed positions so that he could play with her clit.

"What are you doing?"

"Happy hour," he told her.

"Two-fers, Sir?"

In response, he toyed with her, fucking her cunt, tweaking her clitoris, moving his finger in and out of her tightest hole. "Nice," he told her when she began to move.

"I haven't recovered from the first."

"I've found you're not the only one who's greedy," he said. "I want you to come when I do."

His cock became turgid.

"Want," she managed.

He sank his finger in to the hilt. He shortened his strokes inside her, increasing the friction.

Despite his intention to only think about her, the strength of his orgasm plowed into him. "Come," he said.

She nodded.

He buried his dick inside her.

With her pussy, she squeezed him, groaning and pushing back against his thrusts until he came, hard. "Damn," he managed, the word more a grunt than intelligible language.

The urgency of his orgasm pushed her over the edge again, and she came right after he did. Under the force, she pushed him out.

"You have learnt a few things."

She shook her head. "That's all you, Sir. I haven't ever come that hard before."

He eased his finger from her, then bent forward to kiss her. "Be right back." He moved away from her only long enough to discard the condom, wash his hands and dampen a washcloth for her. "It's cool," he said by way of warning before pressing the small towel against her.

"Feels good," she said.

He untied the nylon rope but left the cuffs around her wrists. "Let's get you up." He rolled her onto her back. "On second thought…"

"Sir?"

"I'm tempted to get the flogger and work over your front side."

She tensed, then drew in a breath. "If you say so."

"Perfect response." *Perfect sub.* "I think you've had enough." He helped her up. "I like you being a bit helpless," he admitted.

"And I like the way you take care of me when I am."

"Now the rest of it. Close your eyes." He removed the hood and tossed it toward the bag. Her hair was matted down, and the back of her neck was drenched with sweat.

Reece turned on a nightstand lamp and flipped the switch to turn off the overhead light. "Now you can open your eyes."

He wiped a thumb across one of her eyebrows. "You did well."

"It was delicious. I think I'll feel some of those for a week."

"Good. How was the hood?"

"Not as horrible as I thought it might be. I think I let it be bigger in my mind than it turned out to be. And…"

"I'm waiting."

"Kind of like being tied up, it allows me the freedom to let go a little more. I wasn't worried about my expression or hiding tears."

"Tears?" He touched her eyelashes.

"Not from pain."

He froze. "Were you scared?"

"No. Stop. I would have told you. It was just a little overwhelming. But in a good way."

"We won't play with it again. I want to see your expressions, your tears."

"And I'd like you to occasionally allow me to want the freedom it provides."

"Stalemate."

"Not really. It's ultimately your decision."

She was learning. And so was he.

"Are you pleased with me?"

"Always."

The fact that she seemed to ache to make him happy made his gut tighten. Made him wish— Reece shoved away the thought. He'd told her that they wouldn't talk about the past, but it was always there, waiting, a trap threatening to steal pleasure from the present. "Let's get the handcuffs off."

After he'd unfastened them, she rubbed circulation back into her wrists. Then she looked up at him, as if wondering what was next.

"Come here," he said. He plumped some pillows and pulled back the covers.

She crawled across the bed.

As easily as if the separation had never existed, she snuggled into his arms. He held her tight. She didn't need to know she was the only woman he'd ever spent the whole night with.

"I don't think I remembered to say thank you."

"You didn't." Nor did she need to.

"My manners must be buried beneath my delirium."

"I'll forgive you." He soothed her hair back from her face. "And give you a lesson tomorrow to help reinforce my rules."

"Promise?"

He grinned. "You're making me promise to discipline you?"

"Yes. And I will hold you to it."

She turned toward him, hand splayed on his chest. "Thank you."

"That won't get you out of trouble," he said.

"I was hoping it wouldn't."

"What am I going to do with you, Sarah?" When she showed up in his life, common sense went on a testosterone-fueled vacation. The rest of the weekend would be interesting.

He hoped they both survived it.

With the way she moved her hand lower, suddenly he wasn't sure.

CHAPTER FOUR

Downward dog was giving him a few ideas.

"Watching you do yoga is a nice way to wake up," Reece said, rising onto his elbows to get a better look at Sarah. She was wearing her boy shorts and bra. Evidently she'd gone through his pockets. Her hair was as untamed as a Caribbean storm. And she'd never looked more appealing. Wholesome and sensual in one divinely curved package.

She moved into a lotus position, tucked her hair behind her ears then asked, "How long have you been awake?"

"Since plank."

"That's quite a few minutes, Mr McRae."

"And I've enjoyed every second of them. Except for the clothes. I was hoping for naked triangle pose."

"No chance."

"A man and his morning woody can hope."

"A man and his morning woody can order us some coffee before hitting the shower."

"You're a cold, cold woman, Sarah."

"Julien already sent a text message to remind you about the basketball game."

"He sent you a message?"

"I guess he tried you an hour or so ago and got no response. Message sender showed up as Birthday Boy. How the hell does he do that?"

"He takes great delight in doing things that we mere mortals consider impossible."

She shook her head. "Does he ever sleep?"

"Not that I'm aware of. Been the same way since college." He tossed back the covers.

"Wow. That erection is impressive."

"I blame your downward dog."

"When did you become a yoga expert?"

"I have a DVD. Watched it a few dozen times. Hot, bendable woman in a sports bra and bikini bottoms on a Hawaiian beach. What's not to enjoy?"

"You're supposed to practice along with her."

"Watching her got my heart rate up. Finish your workout. Don't mind me."

"Voyeur."

"How could I not be? When you've got a naked woman contorting her body, I'm happy to be a participant."

"Half naked," she corrected.

"Not in my mind." He called room service and asked for a pot of coffee.

Sarah said something, so he asked the attendant to hold on for a moment.

"What are you planning to drink?" Sarah repeated. Then she smiled serenely.

"Make that two pots of coffee," he said before hanging up.

"I would have ordered it myself, but I wanted to let you sleep."

"If there's half-naked gymnastics going on, feel free to wake me up."

She raised her eyebrows. "You really haven't matured."

"That's for wine."

"Shower, McRae."

"Get in here with me."

"We saw what happened when we did that last night."

"How do you feel? Any bruising? Sore muscles?"

"Not a single bruise. The one mark that was there last night is gone."

"I'll do better next time."

"Good." Looking at him with those impossibly big, impossibly green eyes, she added, "I like to touch them afterwards."

Every time she said something like that, he had an immediate physical reaction. "Grab a condom and take care of this problem you caused."

Thirty seconds later, he had her beneath the spray, palms flat on the tile as he fucked her from behind.

He was a gentleman. He let her come first.

"That doesn't, er…mean…"

"Took the edge off," he assured her, turning her to face him. "You'll be riding my dick later."

He heard a knock on the door, followed by, "Room service."

"Since I value my life, I'll get that," he offered.

"Good. Because I can't move."

He grinned.

A second knock followed, and he called out that he'd be right there. He dried off and wrapped a towel around his waist. No doubt he wasn't the first guest to do that. And, this being Julien's party weekend, no doubt Reece wouldn't be the last.

The waiter rolled in a cart with the coffee. It also held two bottles of Scotch. "They were waiting for you at the front desk," the man explained, "so I brought them up. We'd left you a message." He pointed to the light blinking on the phone.

Kennedy.

And a harsh reminder about how the weekend might end. Would end. Reece had no intention of taking her back and exposing himself to that kind of risk again. No matter how sweet the return.

Reece signed the bill and added a generous tip.

He heard the shower turn off.

"Tell me that was the coffee," she said, exiting the bathroom.

She had one towel wrapped around her and she was rubbing her hair with a second. "Something wrong?" she asked. Then she saw the bottles of alcohol. "Would you like me to go now? Say thanks for the beating and the sex?"

"Probably for the best," he said.

She froze.

"But no."

"Look, Reece, Sir... Crap. I don't even know what to call you. Or this. What we're doing." She sank on the edge of the bed. "I didn't expect that this would be easy."

"We agreed to give it until Sunday night."

"And? What then? I'm starting to think that I'll want more."

"We have no trust between us."

"Not true. I trust you."

"You didn't."

She frowned.

"If you had trusted me and what we shared, you would have stayed."

"Enough said. I'll get dressed and..." She inhaled.

Then he saw her shoulders go rigid.

She dropped the towel she'd been using to dry her hair. With more confidence, she started again, "I'll get dressed and see you after your game. I'm not walking away. You want to get rid of me? Send me away."

Fuck. He wasn't sure he could have let her leave, let alone ask her to go.

"Cream in your coffee?" she asked as if nothing untoward had happened. She stood and crossed to the cart. Without waiting for his answer, she poured each of them a cup and added cream.

He took the cup she offered to him. "Thank you."

"My pleasure."

"Look, Sarah…"

"Unless you've changed your mind, unless you'd like to use a safe word, then honor your promise." She raised her cup in his direction in a toast of sorts, then she took a sip.

Reece cursed himself for being an ass.

He was being waited on by the most beautiful woman he'd ever seen. She was offering a few days with no commitment. The trouble was, for him, at one time, anything less than a lifetime wouldn't have been enough.

And now?

Sarah put her cup on the room's small table. Though he was certain she was trying for an air of nonchalance, he saw the way her hand shook, betraying her nerves. He knew he was the cause of it, and he did nothing to reassure her.

Overnight, her dress had fallen on the floor. She picked it up and pulled it over her head, doing a little dance as the material settled into place.

After draining her cup, she sauntered across the room to him. She slipped on her shoes then leaned in to kiss his forehead. "Enjoy your game."

"Sarah."

At the door, she paused and looked back at him. "Sir?"

He shook his head, and she left, quietly closing the door behind her.

His phone rang. He snatched it up and saw that the caller was the Genius of the Known Universe. Julien, clearly. Reece hadn't programmed his friend's name that way.

"We're waiting on you. Unless you're being led around by your overly large dick, get down here."

"Overly large?"

"I provided the condoms. They weren't too big, were they? I didn't believe Sarah, but she insisted."

"I squeezed into them. Restricted the circulation." He ended the call, cutting off Julien's laughter.

Ten minutes later, he met Julien and Kennedy outside at the multi-purpose area adjoining the tennis courts.

Nearby, workers were cleaning the swimming pool and hot tub. There wasn't much activity outside yet, though he heard the distant hum of people who were having breakfast on the patio. Probably not too far from where he'd removed Sarah's panties last night.

As always, Kennedy looked cool and collected. No matter what, even in a bar room brawl, the man kept his movie star good looks untarnished.

Julien could write books on how to live well—a table was lined with water bottles and sports drinks. There was fresh fruit, orange juice and pastries. A cooler contained damp towels, and there was a minibar off to the side. He wore the latest designer basketball shorts and an authentic jersey from one of the California professional basketball teams. His shoes, though…

"I need a better pair of sunglasses," Reece said.

"Neon green is too much?" Julien asked. "Is it because of the sun?"

Kennedy shrugged.

Reece had to be the one to tell the truth. "It's not because of the sun. They're…" *Hideous.*

"They were a gift from Kennedy."

"Athletic shoes? You're involved in athletic shoes now?"

"Among other things. You might want to see the portfolio. How did your evening go?"

"We here to play a game or discuss my sex life?"

"So there is a sex life to discuss." Julien, sharp as always, seized the opening.

Reece caught movement out of the corner of his eye and glanced toward an approaching figure. "Grant?"

"Hey, you made it," Kennedy said, lifting a hand in greeting.

"We managed to get him out of his cave," Julien said. "Had to use Dynamite."

"It's not really a cave," Grant said.

"Close enough. It's near the National Lab. Built into a mountain." Then with the glee of a kid discussing his favorite action hero, Julien added, "Super-secret stuff. It's where all my best things are developed."

"That was specific," Kennedy remarked.

"Damn glad you made it," Reece said, shaking Grant's hand. He looked rumpled, as if he'd slept in his jeans and button-down shirt. "Didn't think you'd ever leave New Mexico."

"I assume you don't mean literal dynamite?" Kennedy asked, showing that he also never missed a detail.

"No. Working name of my plane. Prototype. Can land on the shortest runway. Not quite as good as a helicopter, but not bad. Explosive take-off power."

"Hence the name," Grant supplied.

"Stock available?" Kennedy asked.

"It's still in development."

"Best time to invest."

"It's going to be a success," Grant added. "I've bought in."

"Can we forget business for five minutes?" Reece asked.

"You bet." Kennedy clapped Grant on the back. "We were discussing Reece's sex life."

"Did you say I could buy into your Scotch business?" Reece asked, desperate for a diversion.

"I need a drink." Grant looked at the table in the distance. "What do you have to do to get a drink around here?"

"You been to bed yet?" Reece asked.

"Not to sleep. Julien sent an enticement to get me out of the office."

"Svetlana is definitely a keeper," Julien said.

"Svetlana?" Reece repeated, intrigued. "Russian?"

"Could be. Or not. She was a spy at one time, according to her résumé."

Only a man who loved to hack into foreign intelligence agencies would consider that an asset.

"I'm not sure which country's payroll she was on, but she has a lot of talents. Speaks half a dozen languages. Can pilot anything that has a propeller. I can tell you this… I would do anything she asked. Or, even better, I like it when she tells me to do things."

"I did exactly as she told me," Grant supplied with a grin. "I liked it when she strapped me down with that five-point harness. My new favorite saying is sit down and hang on."

"Which is why you were up all night." Kennedy's tone held a note of admiration.

"See?" Reece asked. "There's no need to discuss my sex life."

"He'd better hope he scored," Julien said. "Because he sucks at Horse."

Grant scoffed. "We always let you win."

The four had been friends since their first year at the University of Texas at Austin. By any definition, they were an odd group, thrown together by student housing and interest in the campus's co-eds.

Reece had won admission because a long-forgotten uncle had attended the university and had a building with his name on it. Kennedy went out of rebellion, mostly. The school made his list because it was renowned for business, and it was about as culturally different from home as he could get and still stay in the country. Julien had graduated in the top ten percent of his Texas high school class and been accepted at colleges all across the country. Since his mother still considered herself a hippie, Austin had appealed to her and she'd influenced him to attend. His mom had even rented an apartment in the city to be near him, which was why he'd moved into student housing.

The biggest surprise was Grant. An interest in engineering and a scholarship had convinced him.

And after the Night of Infamy in their junior year, where no one would confess or rat on the others, they'd all gone to jail, and the four had become lifelong friends.

"Where's my drink?"

"Bloody Mary mix and vodka are in the refrigerator."

Who the hell brought a bar to a basketball court?

"Olives and celery are there as a garnish."

Grant saluted. "Knew I could count on you."

"I hope you packed some different clothes," Julien said.

"Not a damn thing," Grant replied. "Svetlana didn't give me five minutes to get ready. I barely had enough time to back up my files. Still trying to figure out how the hell she got past security."

"I hired her for a reason. You do have a credit card? You can't come to my party in those pants. And that shirt. Is it supposed to be white?"

"When did you get to be such a snob? There's nothing wrong with my clothes."

"Everything's wrong with them. Including the fact you slept in them."

Kennedy lowered his sunglasses. "He didn't sleep."

Julien scowled. "Tell me you have a credit card. Or bill something to your room."

"It's better than the way you usually dress," Grant protested. "But don't worry, I won't embarrass you at your big event tonight."

"I have an extra pair of athletic shoes he can wear," Kennedy offered.

"Yellow?" Reece asked.

Kennedy nodded. "They come in orange, too. And purple."

"Feet that big, you'd see the glow from outer space," Julien said.

"Your airplane can use them as a landing beacon," Kennedy added.

Julien walked toward the makeshift bar, and Grant joined him.

"Anyone else?" Julien called out, pulling out the bottle of vodka.

Since he had Sarah waiting for him, Reece shook his head.

"Kennedy?"

"Got a telephone conference call."

"It's Saturday," Julien said.

"Sunday in Australia," Kennedy replied. "Want to be sure we're prepped for Monday's market opening."

"You're turning into a dull human being," Julien said. "You need some diversions. Something other than stocks, bonds and hedge funds."

"I enjoy my life."

"Since your daddy made you president, you haven't had a day off."

"I'm here now."

"Physically," Julien countered. "You'll be there tonight?"

"Wouldn't miss it."

"If I see you with a cell phone, I'll drop it in a vat of champagne."

"A vat of champagne?" Reece asked.

"A fountain, technically. But a vat sounded more serious."

"Enough of all this," Grant said. "I want to drink until I pass out." After he downed half the beverage in a single guzzle, he sighed. "A little more vodka, this would be perfect. Find I've got an affinity for all things Russian all of a sudden."

Reece walked to the far side of the court and picked up a basketball. "Who's first?" It had been years since he'd been this relaxed. There was nothing like old friendships, picking up where you left off. He could count on any of these men, no matter the situation or time of day. They had a genuine concern for each other's well-being, and he'd be there for any of them, as well.

"You go ahead and warm up while I finish this," Grant said. "You need the practice."

"Big words for a man who's spent the past few years in the bowels of the earth," Kennedy said, bending to tighten his shoelaces. He walked over to join Reece. "Damn, feels like walking on air."

Kennedy had an uncanny instinct when it came to picking winners. His insight was courted by the biggest print and online media outlets, and he did an occasional spot on television, offering investment tips. If he said something was good, it was. His insights had doubled Reece's money over the years. "Send me a pair?"

"You could buy a pair, you cheap bastard."

"I like them, my whole staff will buy them. Size eleven."

"You got the Scotch?"

"Looking forward to sipping it with a fine cigar."

"How's your lady?"

"She's not mine."

"Looks like she wants to be."

"I don't normally give second chances."

"None of us do," Kennedy agreed, pushing back the brim of his baseball cap. Of course it had his family's company logo on the crown. "You're smarter, wiser now. You'll make the right choice."

Reece bounced the ball a few times then aimed and shot.

"Rim shot," Grant observed from his place on the bench. "You need to get it in the basket."

"Thanks, coach."

Reece grabbed the ball and handed it to Kennedy.

The man took about an hour lining up his shot. Reece wondered if his friend ever made a decision without contemplating all the angles.

"For fuck's sake, shoot the goddamn ball," Julien called.

To his credit, Kennedy never seemed to lose his concentration. When he was ready, after bouncing the ball a few more times, he released the shot.

"That's a swish," Grant said.

"You trying out for a job as a sports announcer?" Reece asked.

"Maybe Kennedy could get me an in."

"I might know someone."

"You know everyone," Reece corrected.

"He'd have to leave the cave," Julien added. "And my employ. And I won't give him up easily."

Grant crunched a celery stalk. "I don't know. Having thousands of adoring fans listen to my every word like they do Kennedy's? I could do play-by-play from courtside. Not a bad way to earn a living."

"I've got Svetlana on my payroll," Julien crowed. "She's at your disposal."

Grant dropped his head. "There goes my second career."

"Saw a movie once," Kennedy said. "Russian woman had sex with a man. Then she broke his neck with her thighs."

Grant grinned. "I'll take one for the team."

Julien put down his glass and picked up the basketball. He landed a basket on the first try. The ball bounced back toward him, and he tossed it to Grant.

"I'm drinking." That didn't stop him from palming the ball.

"So am I," Julien responded.

In boots and his rumpled dress clothes, still holding the remnants of a cocktail, he wandered over.

Reece offered to hold the drink.

Grant shook his head. He set up the throw using the glass's rim as a guide then shot the ball. It hung up on the rim then tipped in.

"Fuck me," Reece said.

"Man's a professional," Kennedy observed. "Not sure if I'm talking about drinker or basketball player."

"Lucky shot?" Julien asked.

"You've been sandbagging," Reece said. "All these years."

"Don't like to brag. Played pickup in high school." He saluted them with the glass.

"We should play teams." Kennedy nodded. "I'll pick Grant."

"And leave me with McRae?" Julien asked. "No fucking way."

"Feelings getting hurt here," Reece protested.

Kennedy shrugged. "No room for feelings in basketball. Not when it comes to winning."

"I'm out," Grant said. "Play on, gents. I'm headed to bed." He got a refill from the mini-fridge, then called out. "Will Svetlana be at your party?"

"I'll make sure of it."

"I could die a happy man tonight."

"You might," Kennedy warned. "Remember that movie."

"It would be a hell of a way to go," Julien mused.

With a wave, Grant strolled toward the hotel.

Several workers were dragging wooden chaises longues to the areas of the beach that had already been groomed. Others followed with big umbrellas. Several women in bikinis walked past, carrying tote bags and towels. All Reece could think about was the woman upstairs, waiting for him.

The game of Horse began in earnest. Kennedy took the first shot, a ridiculous underhand throw, which he landed, but Julien and Reece both missed.

"Next?" he offered.

Julien accepted the ball and went for a lay-up. Reece missed. Kennedy nailed it.

"You're already an O," Kennedy noted.

"Nothing wrong with your powers of observation." It only took a few more rounds for him to be thoroughly humiliated.

"Don't feel too bad," Julien said. "You still get to wear the big boy condoms."

Kennedy helpfully added, "Not everyone can brag about that."

"See you tonight."

He left his two friends to battle for Horse supremacy. Grant definitely had the right idea. Grab a cocktail and head upstairs to bed.

As he walked through the lobby, he passed a jewelry store and a women's clothing boutique. There were a couple of dresses that would look good on Sarah. One, in particular, had an open back and plunging neckline.

When they'd been together, he'd enjoyed taking her shopping. He loved watching her model for him, turning slowly at times, and other times doing quick pirouettes that made a hem flare. No matter her mood, he'd been captivated by her.

On the ninth floor, he went to his room, took a quick shower and changed his clothes before going to her room. He knocked on the door and waited. When she didn't respond, he knocked a second time. Hearing no sounds from inside, he pounded. "Damn it, Sarah!"

"Looking for me?"

He turned. She'd just exited the elevator and was walking toward him, wearing a fluffy white robe and slippers.

"I had a massage," she said. "I figured you'd be with your friends for a while, and I needed to work out some kinks from last night."

He pointed to a spot on the floor in front of him. "Come here."

Head held high, she did.

"I'm still here, Reece. You haven't scared me away."

This woman. Damn it. Damn *her*. He wanted her. Wanted not to want her. "Get dressed."

"I didn't mean to upset you."

He refused to admit that she had.

She fished her key card from her pocket "Do you mind if I shower first?"

"Make it a quick one."

The light on the door turned green, and he heard the subtle sound of the lock releasing.

"Are you coming in?"

"Yes."

He placed his hand on her hip as she walked through the entrance. Then he slammed the door closed behind them. "Stop." He took hold of her and spun her to face him.

"Reece?"

He backed her against the door. "Undo that belt."

Her mouth parted slightly, she did as he had ordered.

"Now get it off."

She shrugged from the robe and allowed it to pool on the tile.

This wasn't about submission and Dominance, he knew. It was about them. About what he needed from her. It was more than total compliance, it was about her willingness.

Seeing it there, in her eyes, he bent to claim her mouth. He'd never desired a woman like he wanted her.

Instead of standing there, she responded, lifting her arms, wrapping them around his neck, seeking his strength.

He accepted everything she offered and, with his tongue plunging into the softness of her mouth, demanded more.

She met him thrust for thrust, giving, offering, yielding.

When he ended the kiss, they were both breathless. She boldly met his gaze. "I'm still not scared."

A tremor shook her voice, betraying her lie despite the brave front. "You should be."

"Don't underestimate me."

"All along, Sarah, my mistake lay in overestimating you."

"I'm not the same woman."

She was better. Stronger. More determined. All the more reason to be wary. "Take your shower," he told her.

He stepped aside. As she passed, she trailed her fingers along his arm.

After picking up her discarded robe, he followed her. He tossed the garment on the bathroom floor, near the soiled towels.

While she showered, he went to her closet. He selected an ankle-length sleeveless dress with a criss-cross back. He particularly liked the row of buttons up the front. The question was, how many of them would he allow her to fasten?

In record time, she rejoined him.

"Leave the bottom three buttons open," he instructed, handing her the teal-colored dress.

"That's one of my favorites." She slipped it on. "How does it look?"

"Unfasten another button," he said. "I want to see your knees."

With a nod, she did as he said.

"Better."

Sarah removed a clip from her hair and fluffed the length around her shoulders.

"Beautiful."

She pushed her feet into a pair of sandals and grabbed a small purse. "I take it we're going somewhere?"

"We are."

"Breakfast?" she guessed, following him into the elevator. "My coffee has about worn off."

"After we're done."

She frowned but didn't question him.

In the lobby, Julien was holding court.

"Nice shoes," Sarah told him.

"They'll be available in ladies' sizes this fall," he said.

"Want to be our spokesperson?" Kennedy asked Julien.

"I'm wearing them, aren't I? That ought to be worth a million dollars to your bottom line."

"It would be if the press were here," Kennedy lamented.

"And none of us would have nearly this much fun," Julien said.

Reece knew that, except for annual BondStreet corporate gatherings, Julien fought to keep the press away from his life and business. When people sent in an RSVP to one of his functions, they also had to include a signed confidentiality statement, swearing to keep all the event details private. Attendees even agreed not to publish pictures of the festivities on their own social media accounts. Still, rumors swirled, and everyone expected an intrepid paparazzo or two to charter a boat or helicopter to spy on the festivities. "If you'll excuse us," Reece said.

"Don't do anything we wouldn't," Julien said.

Two women, tanned, toned, dressed in only bathing suits as if they were getting ready to compete in a beauty pageant, walked over and flanked Julien.

Kennedy shook his head and extracted a ringing phone from his pocket.

"Last call until you're back on the mainland," Julien warned as Kennedy answered.

"What kind of phone is that?" Sarah asked.

"You'll know in about three months," Julien replied.

"Prototype?"

He nodded. "It will be the hottest thing on the market this spring."

One of the ladies left Julien and went toward Kennedy.

"Fickle," Julien said.

Shaking his head, Reece guided Sarah toward the boutique.

"I've heard he hasn't gone on a date in over a year," Sarah said.

"Julien doesn't have time for distractions. He prefers intellectual discussion, or maybe someone to play his latest video game."

"Maybe that's what they want to do," Sarah said, looking back.

"I'm sure it is," Reece agreed. He was certain that was why they'd shown up as close to naked as possible.

"Are we going shopping?" Sarah asked when they neared the boutique.

"There's something I'd like you to try on for tonight's party."

"I brought—"

He glanced at her, and she shut up.

A second later, she added, "What I mean is, I'd love to try it on, Sir."

Inside the store, he pointed out the dress that had caught his interest.

"Excellent choice," the saleswoman said as she eyed Sarah. She thumbed through the hangers to find the right size before leading the way to the changing room.

Reece followed along.

"Let me know if there's anything I can do to help," the woman said.

"We're fine," he assured her. "Thank you."

The woman opened her mouth, but then shut it again. Without any further protest, she left them alone.

"Really, Reece, I can manage on my own," Sarah informed him.

"I'm sure you can."

"But you're not going to let me?"

"I want to be here."

"In that case, I'd love to have you as my lady's maid."

"Don't push it."

She grinned. "What girl wouldn't want one of the world's most famous CEOs to take off her clothes?"

The oversized room was luxurious, as he would have expected. Three full-length mirrors were affixed to the walls. And a padded bench completed the space.

Reece closed and locked the door before capturing the bottom of Sarah's dress. He swept it up, pulled it off her then tossed the teal material toward the bench.

"Took care of that," she said, voice hardly over a whisper.

He liked the look of her, naked, except for sandals, only inches from him. Though she'd showered, the faint scent of a floral essential oil lingered on her skin.

"Bend over," he instructed. "Grab your ankles. I want to see if you have any red marks from last night."

"There aren't any. I looked. Besides, you saw me naked in the shower."

He folded his arms.

Immediately she bent and took hold of her ankles.

"Spread your legs a little. Just a couple of inches," he said, placing a hand on her back.

When she complied, he fingered her pussy.

"I like your version of shopping, Sir," she said with a soft sigh.

"It's the hands-on approach," he agreed. Once he felt her orgasm begin to build, he moved his hand and said, "Try on the dress."

He took it from the hanger and held it for her.

"You really do have a mean streak," she protested.

The material skimmed her body, clinging to her curves in all the right ways. It was revealing, yet classy, feminine.

"It's…" She turned sideways to glance in the mirror. "Risqué."

"Sensational," he added, drawing a finger down her spine. "I like this part." The dress she'd worn last night had covered less skin, but this seemed more provocative. "And this." He traced the V between her breasts.

"I think you can see my toes."

He shook his head. "It's not that low-cut."

In the mirror, she caught his gaze. "You don't think it's too much?"

"I think it's perfect."

She examined herself from a few more angles. "You have a talent for picking out things that suit me."

"We're not done yet."

"Oh?"

He sat on the bench, grabbed her wrist and tugged her over his lap. Breath whooshed out of her, leaving her a little limp. Before she could recover, he flipped up her dress, exposing her buttocks. "This dress will most definitely work," he said.

"Do you only think about one thing, Mr McRae?"

"Several, actually."

She squirmed. "Spanking me and—"

"You can think about the others for a while."

"Fucking me?"

"That's one of them, yes." He brought his hand down hard on her right butt cheek.

She yelped, more from shock than pain, he was sure. The sound echoed off the ceiling and sent a ripple of satisfaction through him. "You were right. There wasn't a red mark. Now there is."

He liked the sight of it, his mark on her skin.

"Thank you."

Reece shrugged off the sudden feeling of possessiveness and helped her up.

While she changed, he sought out the saleswoman, made the purchase and instructed her to have the package delivered to his room.

Sarah met him near the shop's entrance. As the idea for his next stop tumbled through his mind, he realized that he intended to test himself as well as her.

"Let's go next door."

Outside the door, she paused and frowned. "It's a jewelry store."

"They have chokers," he said. "You can pretend it's a collar."

CHAPTER FIVE

For Sarah, time seemed to slow. "I'm confused," she said. "I thought we only agreed to the weekend together."

"We did."

"So…" She searched his face, looking for something, anything to give her an idea of what he was thinking.

His eyes, so blue and enigmatic, were unreadable.

She had spent the first few weeks after she'd run from him feeling grateful that she'd gotten away. Then she'd spent a few months trying to sort out her life and re-establish her business. And when she'd started to date again, she'd begun to see Reece in a different light, and she'd started to regret her decision. For the past few weeks, she'd been consumed with the idea of seeing him, getting over him, moving on with her life.

But after last night, she had realized that was impossible.

Everything she'd once felt for him was still there, the passion, the energy, the joy. The sex had magnified it.

The fear, though, if she was honest, was worse than it had been two years ago.

He'd changed as much as she had. Part of her wished that

he was the man he had been before. Kind, caring, willing to do anything to soothe her.

This man was harsher, feelings and reactions buried beneath the hurt.

Despite that, she was facing the fact that she wanted more time with him.

And she recognized he had all the power.

She had no doubt that he desired her. Though he hadn't said so, she'd be willing to bet he'd scene with her, at least until he found someone else.

That thought stung.

How the hell had she thought she could do this?

It had all seemed so simple when she wasn't standing only inches from him, her body humming from a heady, dangerous combination of pheromones. "Help me out here. I don't understand why you want me to wear a choker for only one night."

"It would look sensational with your dress."

The plunging neckline did call out for jewelry. "So that's all?"

"Let's try it out. We'll go in, select something together, and I'll put it on you before we go down to Julien's party. You'll attend as my submissive, for the whole world to see."

A wicked combination of desire and apprehension unfurled deep in her stomach. He'd said he would test her. And this felt like a significant one. Carefully she asked, "Can we talk about what that means to you?"

"If anyone asks, you admit you're my submissive."

"I think your friends already know, or at least they suspect."

"They do."

"No one else's opinion would matter."

"True."

"Now I'm really puzzled. Is there any specific behavior you demand from me?"

"The same courtesy you usually show me."

She was aware of others walking by, but no one seemed to notice them. And why would they? Julien's guests valued their privacy, and most of them were absorbed with their own lives.

"No kneeling by your side while you feed me treats from your plate or give me sips from your champagne?"

"Now that you mention it…"

She scowled.

"Sarah, when have I ever asked something like that from you? Some couples may enjoy that. But I certainly don't demand that kind of behavior. It might be entertaining at a play party in Houston, if we both agreed to it."

"I still don't get it. How would it change anything between us?"

"That's my point."

"Could you be a little less obscure? I feel as if we're speaking different languages here."

"It changes nothing, except what happens inside your mind. It's a commitment from you to me."

"But only for tonight."

"Only for tonight."

"You're paying for it?"

"I am."

"Then I want a really nice one."

"I want you to have a big, thick one. I want it to be so heavy that you to have a difficult time holding your head up."

She started to object, but then she saw it, a lessening of the tension next to his eyes. It was a contradiction to his serious tone. She wondered, over the years, how many times she had missed the subtle clues as to what he was thinking.

"As long as it's on your credit card, you can get me whatever you want." Even as she said it, adrenaline flooded her system. This wasn't the same as the collar she'd found in his drawer. It meant nothing as far as a lifetime commitment, but some of her old doubts were there, swirling.

He offered his arm and she took it. "We're looking for a choker," he told the gentleman behind the counter.

"Yes, sir. Anything specific? Gold? Silver? Platinum?"

Reece looked at her and quirked his right eyebrow.

"Silver or platinum."

"My lady has good taste."

"White gold would also be okay," she said.

The clerk pulled out a few choices. A few were delicate—a couple were stout enough to hold a good-sized pendant.

"Anything appeal to you?" Reece asked.

"Whatever you like, Sir."

Reece pointed to one and told the man they'd like to try it on.

"Excellent choice. White gold."

The necklace was wide and there was no price tag, which told her a lot.

"Lift your hair."

When she did, Reece fastened the choker around her neck and settled it into place. "How's that? Too tight?" His voice teased her ear, warm and reassuring.

She took a deep breath and released her hair. "No. It's fine."

The clerk instantly offered a handheld mirror.

Reece was still behind her, and she saw them together, with the choker snuggled against her throat, right above her collarbone.

The expression on his face—pleasure and triumph—thrilled her. She didn't take it as gloating, she took it as masculine pride.

"What do you think?" the salesman asked.

"What do you think?" she asked Reece, their gazes locked in the mirror.

"I think it's stunning."

"So do I." She exhaled a shaky breath.

"Would you like to have it?"

"I—"

"What?" His tone was tight.

"I'm sure it costs too much."

The clerk named a figure that had a comma in it.

"That would pay my mortgage for a couple of months. Like six months, really."

"Any objection beyond the price?"

She turned to look at him, placing the mirror face down on the counter, aware of the clerk's interest. "Reece, this is ridiculous. I may only wear it once."

"Any other objections? Emotional ones? Mental ones?"

"Nothing other than the fact that it's too expensive." She looked at the clerk. "Can we see something less pricey? Maybe in silver?"

"Sarah."

She faced Reece and realized her error. His lips were pressed together. "I…" She paused. "I'm still not very good at this, am I? If it pleases you, Sir, I'd be honored to wear it."

"Lift your hair." He removed the choker.

"Reece, I apologize."

"Wrap it up," he instructed the clerk.

The man smiled. "It looks lovely on you," he said to Sarah. "It's beautiful."

A few minutes later, they left the store with Reece carrying the bag.

"At least I didn't piss you off enough that you didn't buy it."

"Good thing," he replied.

She was tempted to offer to go back to the room,

anything to get away from his hostility, but figuring that would annoy him even more, she kept her mouth shut.

"Breakfast?"

"I'm starving," she said.

They went to another outdoor restaurant. Since they were later than most people, they had the place to themselves. The hostess seated them near a fountain. After promising to return with coffee, she left them alone.

A grackle landed on the edge of the fountain, making its obnoxious jeeb-jeeb-jeeb sound.

"That's one of the ways I know I'm in the Keys," she said.

A bus person shooed away the bird. It left for thirty seconds before returning.

A waitress brought coffee and took their orders.

"Look, Reece, I'm sorry. I should have spoken with you, not the clerk. I was wrong. I get that you're angry. And I don't blame you." She put her hand on the table, palm up, beseeching him. "I didn't run. I'm still here. I didn't freak out. Well, except for the idea of spending so much of your money."

"You mentioned that it would pay your mortgage for several months. It occurs to me I don't even know where you live. I assumed you weren't struggling financially, but I could be wrong."

Suddenly she realized how big the gulf was between them. It wasn't a matter of her showing up, apologizing, getting a spanking and pretending that everything was fine, as if they'd never been apart.

They might have agreed to keep the past behind them, but she was beginning to believe that was impossible. She had the unfair advantage of having been able to keep up with him, his successes, his struggles. "I am doing okay. I live in Colorado."

"Colorado?"

"It was a big move," she said. "Totally different from Houston. I thought I was going to freeze that first winter. With the humidity, Houston can feel cold, but not like that. The first time it was thirty below with the wind chill, I booked a vacation to Key West."

"Why Colorado?"

"My college roommate was living in Denver, and geographically, culturally, it was light years away from Texas. I thought I'd stay until I figured out what I wanted to do, but I fell in love with Golden. I bought a town home in Golden, near the School of Mines. Amazing views. I can ride my bike almost any place."

"As long as it's not snowing."

"True enough."

"And you still have your business?"

She shook her head. "I sold that one. Not for much money, but enough to help me get re-established. I've done quite well with the new venture, thanks to the skills I learnt working for you. I found a niche."

"I'm not surprised."

When she realized he had no clue what type of business she was doing, she said, "I own a virtual assistant company. We cater to small business owners, entrepreneurs mainly, people who don't really want someone in their office all the time or can't afford a number of different employees. We do remote payroll, accounting, bookkeeping, HR services."

He nodded.

"What makes us unique is that we also handle things such as social media, web updates, answering phones, PR, marketing campaigns, mailings. We provide one point of contact, and I have dozens of really talented people who work for me, some full-time, some part-time. We have about a dozen who freelance. One stop, one bill."

"Brilliant. Does Julien know about it?"

"No. He was your friend. I didn't think it was fair to ask him for business advice."

He sat back and pushed his coffee away.

"I know. Nothing I did was fair."

"I didn't say it."

"You didn't have to. I can see it in your eyes. And you're right to think it. What I did was monumentally wrong. I don't deserve forgiveness. Nothing I do will change the past."

"Would you like a hair shirt now, or later?"

Her half-smile faded quickly.

Their food arrived and she slathered her waffle with butter and syrup. "I'm on vacation," she said with a shrug. "And carbs make me feel better."

"No judgment from me."

"Says he who is eating a vegetarian egg white omelet."

They were finishing their meal when North Star and Magenta paused at their table. "Loved the set-up," Magenta said. "I think I could get accustomed to this young man doing my bidding." She traced his jawline.

North Star grinned. "Had a hard time sitting this morning," he confessed.

"Too much information," Sarah said.

"You may want to put a salve on his marks when you finish with him," Reece said. "Arnica works well. I prefer a cream to an ointment for my subs."

Stunned, Sarah curled her hands around the mug, unable to believe they were having this conversation in public with others nearby.

"What did you use?"

"My belt. This one." North Star fingered it and grinned. "Bites like a sonofabitch."

"Check with Kennedy Aldrich. He might have packed some extra toys."

"Will do," Magenta said. "Didn't know he was a kinkster."

"He's a Dungeon Master at a club on the east coast. And adult toys are big business. He's invested in some companies."

"Makes sense," Magenta said. "Shall we, North Star?" She looped his tie around her hand and pulled him in closer.

"Yes, Mistress."

The two moved on.

"I didn't realize Kennedy is a DM."

"He also does some one-on-one instruction. Taught me how to use the looped flogger."

"When I first met him, he remarked on my training."

"He knows a few details. Nothing to make you too uncomfortable."

"About you wanting to collar me?"

He nodded.

"What did he say?"

"Two years ago, he showed up as one of my best friends. Yesterday, after seeing the efforts you went to, to get here, he reminded me that there's a difference between fear and cowardice."

"What do you think?"

"I'm wondering where that line is."

What would it be like if the situation were reversed, if he'd walked out on her? Would she be quick to forgive? Would she try again? And if she did, would doubt linger, gnawing at the edges of their happiness?

He'd placed the bag from the jeweler's in the middle of the table, next to a small flower vase, ensuring that she'd have to look at it through the whole meal.

He'd teased her about wearing a hair shirt. Maybe she was. Maybe she deserved it.

"You're scowling."

"I don't like what I'm thinking about," she admitted.

"Which is?"

"The shoe being on the other foot, so to speak. Imagining what I did to you."

"Uncomfortable?"

"Very."

"I could try wearing yours," he said.

"Not sure you'd look good in heels." She smiled because that was what he'd intended. But there really was no possible way to apologize for the damage she'd caused.

"Forget it. For now."

Who knew it would be Reece who encouraged her to move away from the self-criticism? "You're more magnanimous than I am," she said.

"More focused on the moment, maybe."

From their vantage point, she saw Magenta walk past, still leading her sub by the tie. "Are they married?"

"No. They live in separate towns. So nothing beyond occasional hook-ups at events."

"I think after last night, it might become a little more serious. But really, with names like those, they seem to belong together. Who puts Magenta and North Star on a birth certificate? I mean, beyond movie stars?"

"Not their parents. Alternate identities. When they come here, they leave their real lives behind. Magenta runs a publicly traded company and if her wild streak were known, her board of directors would vote her out. He's an investigative reporter, network television. One of the only members of the press allowed at the event, but only because he left his credentials on the mainland. I'm surprised you don't recognize him."

"I don't watch much TV."

Reece signed the check.

"I'm surprised they were so open...about what they did last night."

"They knew we were a friendly audience."

"Well, they're not hiding it now, either."

"Tonight, Sarah, everyone will know about the nature of our relationship."

The waffle sat heavy in her stomach. "You're trying to make me nervous. Test me again." See if she was worthy of trust?

He stood and pulled back her chair. "We've only got a couple of hours before getting ready for the big party."

"I heard a rumor that a cheerleader will be popping out of his cake."

"Probably more like an entire squad," he said.

"I've got a few ideas on how to pass the time."

"Oh?" He pulled her against him and she willingly went. It didn't matter who was watching. The only thing that mattered was him.

"Yesterday you promised me a lesson to help reinforce your rules."

"So I did. Do you want it here or upstairs?"

She shivered, and it wasn't from the breeze dancing off the ocean. The things he said scored a direct hit on her libido. "You wouldn't dare."

"I spanked you in the restaurant last night," he reminded her.

A chill danced through her. She remembered. "Upstairs," she said. "Stat."

"Excellent choice."

He smiled, and it was as if the world tilted back into its correct position. Reece mattered to her. And she was realizing that his reputation as the Iceman was correct. He never yelled or got really angry. His moods were not mercurial. But she much preferred him when he was being warm and loving.

"My room," he said.

The choice was intentional, she knew. That was where the toys were, and she'd be in his space, not her own.

"What was the transgression?" he asked when they were sealed in the silence of his room.

"I forgot to say thank you after our scene."

He placed the bag with her choker next to the television. Then he took two steps toward her.

She stood her ground, looking at him, waiting for him.

"What's the proper punishment?"

Sarah thought. "Well, I had a flogging. Which I enjoyed."

While he waited for her answer, he folded his arms over his chest—on purpose, she was sure. He suddenly looked much fiercer.

"And you gave me a paddling."

"Did you like that?"

"Yes. I really liked it."

"What about it appealed to you?"

"The impact…" She tried to find the words to describe the way it had utterly mastered her. "It's only in one spot, but the pain is blunt, so I really felt it. Then… There's the sound of it." Sarah rubbed her forearms. "Unmistakable. Very intimidating. It sounds hollow, and it reverberates. You gave me fewer strokes, which I'm not saying is something I want, but the interlude feels more heightened because it's shorter. It's… I'm rambling."

"I like it. Tell me more."

"The whole experience is sublime."

"Agreed. The leather paddle sounds even better."

"That's in the bag."

"It is," he agreed.

"Shall I fetch it?" she offered.

"Is that what you want?"

"Honestly?" She shook her head.

"Then?"

"After what North Star said… I want to try your belt."

"Take it off me, then."

In an instant, they'd gone from teasing to a scene. The way he looked at her, spoke to her, changed something inside her. Her blood seemed to thicken in her veins, and sounds became amplified. Her reaction was always immediate. Palpable.

She reached for his belt.

"On your knees, Sarah." That tone… Implacable. Confident of her compliance.

"Yes, Sir." She knelt. When nerves assailed her, her fingers felt like thumbs, and it took her a couple of attempts to release the buckle.

The leather hissed when she pulled it from his belt loops.

"Put it on the bed then stand up and take off your clothes."

Her tummy was in knots as she laid out the belt then removed her dress. She stood before him, naked.

"Present your body to me, Sarah."

She put her hands behind her neck and arched her back to thrust her breasts toward him. Then she placed her feet shoulder-width apart.

"What's the proper number of strokes?"

"You know I hate that question, right?"

"Which is why I ask it."

Too many, and she might be in for some real pain. If she named a number too low, he might double it to teach her a lesson. Worse, she might be frustrated if she didn't reach the endorphin high that she longed for. "Eight."

"Why eight?"

"It's the number of letters in thank you."

"Nine," he said. "One for the space between the words."

"Perfect."

He dragged over a chair and sat. "Over my knee."

This was what she craved. The connection, skin to skin, the intimacy. She loved the cross and bondage, but this was even better.

Drawing a few breaths, she positioned herself.

He juggled her so that her ass was more prominent, and he trapped her legs between his.

"Grab hold of the chair and don't let go."

"This seems serious, Sir." Enough that her breaths were already ragged.

"It's meant to reinforce your manners."

"It will."

He rubbed her thighs and buttocks. "Your skin was meant for this."

Her body was made for him.

"Because of yesterday's paddling, you'll feel this more keenly."

"Good."

"Be careful of what you wish for."

But she wasn't. She very much realized the clock was ticking, and she wanted to seize every possible experience.

He reached for the belt and folded it in half.

"Spell for me."

He blazed the belt above her knees. Screaming, she arched and let go of the chair.

"A little unexpected?" he asked.

"Fuck," she whispered.

"Spell," he reminded her, relentlessly.

"T."

"How many more to go?"

"Can we spell thanks, instead, Sir?"

"I warned you to be careful of what you asked for."

Maybe she should have heeded his advice.

He waited while she struggled back into position and was

breathing normally again. The moment she relaxed her body, he seared the top of her buttocks.

She tried to roll to her side, but he tightened his grip. "That thing hurts," she said.

"What letter are we on?"

"H, Sir."

"And I asked how many more to go?"

The pain receded, leaving peace in its wake. "Seven, Sir."

"Let me know when you're ready."

She settled back into place. Had he always been this courteous? She knew, from recent experiences with other men, that not everyone was this in tune with her. "Ready. Thank you, Sir."

The third strike landed in the middle of her buttocks. It didn't feel as harsh. She wondered if that was because he'd used less force after she'd remembered to thank him, or whether her body's natural high was kicking in. "A," she said. "Thank you."

As she relaxed, he responded by picking up the pace.

They fell into a rhythm that left her breathless.

"Sarah?"

For a minute she didn't respond.

"Where are we, Sarah?"

Reece stroked her back with a gentle, feathery touch. She realized he was reaching out to her, making sure they were connected. A few times, he'd allowed her to get lost in a scene, but not today. "O, Sir?" she guessed.

"Last one."

Reflexively, she tensed her muscles. Then she forced herself to relax.

"Very good," he told her.

He laid the leather to her again, and she gasped. "U. Thank you, Sir."

She realized that he hadn't touched her sexually. But she was getting aroused, nonetheless.

"You did well."

Sarah remained where she was, feeling the burn in her thighs and buttocks, enjoying the strength of him, beneath her, the reassurance of his grip on her waist.

After a few seconds, he stroked her between her legs.

"Sir, I'm…" she mewled.

"Hot and sexy?"

"I…"

He slid a finger inside her.

"I'm close." She squirmed, trying to get away. If he didn't let her orgasm, there was no way she could remain in this position.

"Come," he said, pushing three fingers deep inside her while pressing his thumb pad against her clit.

"Reece! Sir!" Thrashing her head, she climaxed.

Then, suddenly, she wasn't capable of thought.

He scooped her up and held her tight. There was no place she'd rather be.

By small measures, awareness returned. She felt his shirt beneath her cheek, his strong arms wrapped around her. She breathed in his power, savored the way he'd claimed her.

No one else had ever touched the part of her that he did.

"How about a bath?" he offered minutes later when she started to ease away from him.

"Sounds delicious."

"I'll have some bubbly sent up."

"Are we celebrating something?"

"That, and rewarding your behavior," he said.

She wriggled around to face him. "So what are we celebrating?"

"Your upcoming introduction to anal sex."

Her stomach plummeted. "You do that on purpose."

He raised an eyebrow in mock innocence.

"Catch me off guard," she clarified. "I'm relishing my orgasms and you're raising the bar on what you expect from me."

"True enough."

"Have you always done that? Or is it that part of my test?"

"Tell me what you think."

"You've always kept me on edge, guessing." She frowned. "You stay one step ahead of me."

"It's a Dom's responsibility. I don't want to be predictable or bore you."

"Not likely," she said.

He jostled her from his lap. "Go turn on the bath water while I call room service."

Twenty minutes later, she had her hair pinned up and was relaxing in the oversized tub when he came in with a flute of sparkling wine.

She sat up to accept the glass. The first sip tickled her nose. "Delicious. Thank you." She put the glass down and let her head rest on the built-in pillow again. "Between the massage, the orgasm, and the spanking, I feel like a limp noodle," she said, closing her eyes.

"Good."

Sarah heard sounds of him moving around and, interested in what he was doing, she opened her eyes. His shoes were beneath the counter, along with his shorts. He was pulling his shirt over his head. "Whatever you're thinking, I like it," she said.

"Move over."

"You're coming in?" Anticipation swirled inside her, deliciously.

"If you'll make some room." He dropped his shirt to the floor.

His cock was thick and erect, and her mouth watered.

135

Everything about him turned her on. "You're one fine specimen, Mr McRae." Though she'd come within the last half hour, she wanted him again.

He stepped into the tub and sat across from her, splashing some water over the rim. He ran a damp hand over his face, then regarded her. *Hungrily?*

"Want me in your lap?" she offered.

"No. We can both wait until tonight."

"But…"

"A little denial will do you good, keep you on edge."

She closed her mouth. When his chin was set at that angle, there was no arguing with him.

He picked up his glass and took a deep drink.

"I need a bath like this," she said. And a man like him to share it.

"You don't have one in Colorado?"

"The complex has an outdoor hot tub, but for personal conversations and privacy, it's hard to beat this."

"Do you miss Houston?"

"I like Colorado," she said, looking at him. She wondered if his question meant anything, or if it was just idle curiosity, conversation making. Just in case, she wanted to be sure that he understood. "There's nothing like hiking in the mountains. But there's a lot about Houston that I miss."

"I'm guessing August isn't one of them?"

She grinned. "Well, August is a good excuse for a mint julep." She let her smile fade. "The nice thing about my business is that I can do it from anywhere. I don't have an outside office. If I can grab an Internet connection and phone signal, I can work anywhere."

"That also means you probably never take vacations."

"This is my first in two years. I'm a little twitchy. Weekends aren't always as busy as weekdays, but honestly, a lot of entrepreneurs don't look at the clock or calendar before having a brilliant idea or calling to demand an update on a project."

"Do you get lonely?"

"I have friends."

"That wasn't the question."

"Doesn't everyone?" she asked. She looked at him and allowed her honesty to pour out. "I miss you, Reece, and the way we'd brainstorm and strategize. I'm really at a frustrating point in my business."

"Go on."

Since he was sitting up, paying close attention to her, she continued. "It's easy to be an adviser to my clients. I can easily see what they need, when they need to hire, or fire, or launch a marketing campaign." She blew out a breath, moving a wisp of hair out of the way. "But I'm so busy, I'm not sure what I need to do next. Hire another assistant? Spin off work to someone else? Look for a buyer? Let some clients go? I'm poised for growth, but I'm not sure how to get there, what's the next logical thing. I keep thinking I need a board of directors. I know there are some coaching groups out there that provide that service, but I want something a little more personal." She took a drink. "Probably more than you wanted to know."

"You're right that you need an adviser. I know people you can talk to. If you're interested in selling afterwards, Kennedy or I can hook you up with experts on business valuations."

"Do you no longer do that?"

"I do."

Unspoken words hung between them. Yes, he provided business valuations. But not for her.

"If you're interested in trying to franchise, Kennedy works with a company who can handle that," he continued.

"I appreciate it." She'd hoped for more, maybe that he'd

ask questions and give her real suggestions, like he had in the past. His responses were another reminder of what she'd walked away from. What would her life have been like if she hadn't let fear threaten the future? Maybe their relationship wouldn't have lasted, but she had no way of knowing that.

"Can I take you to dinner before Julien's party?"

"I'd like that."

"I want you on your knees," he said.

She smiled. "I'm glad you changed your mind."

"It's not what you think."

Kneeling, she straddled him. She began to lower herself toward his cock but was stopped when he clamped his hands on her waist.

"Stay still."

"I think you want me as much as I want you, Sir."

"No doubt."

"So...?"

"Hand me the shaving cream and the razor."

She scowled.

"I told you yesterday I intended to remove that strip of pubic hair."

"I was hoping you'd forgotten that."

"The shaving cream, Sarah."

She reached over and grabbed the small metal can. He held out a hand, and she dispensed a small amount of the foam into his palm.

He rubbed it into her pubic hair then rinsed his hand.

"This is a little personal."

"Not as personal as having me up your ass."

"About that—"

"Razor?"

She handed it to him.

With a few deft swipes, he left her pubic area bare.

"I think it looks odd," she said.

"Sexy," he countered.

"If you say so, Sir."

"You're learning." He rinsed her off, then said, "Get your cunt over here so I can kiss it."

The words, crude and unexpected, shot an illicit thrill through her. And figuring out how to do as he instructed took some creativity.

She stood then placed a hand on the back wall and curved the other around a safety bar on the side wall. She put one foot on the bathtub's rim, the other next to his body. She leaned forward, supporting herself as she lowered her shaved pussy toward his face.

He put one hand on her hip to help guide her and he parted her labia with the other.

"This is tricky."

"I don't always ask for what's easiest," he reminded her.

"I'd say that was a fact, Sir."

He licked her clit and she pulled back.

"Easy," he warned.

She lowered herself again.

"This time, stay there."

She nodded.

He licked, sucked, kissed.

She moaned. Staying still became more and more difficult. "Sir!"

He continued, but she was mindful of his earlier statement that she had to wait for her next orgasm.

"Sir? Reece? I think…" She jerked, fighting off the climax.

Then, when she was on the edge, he took her by the waist and held her away from him.

Shudders of frustration chased through her. "You've never done that to me before," she said.

"Imagine how hard you're going to come later," he said.

"I can come now *and* later."

"Choose. Now *or* later? Consider your answer. Do you really want this to be your last orgasm of the day?"

Defeated, she sighed.

"Good decision."

He climbed out of the tub, shucked off the water then held out a towel for her. She reached to take it, but he said, "Allow me."

Using slow circles, he dried her.

"I think I'm supposed to do that for you."

"We make our own rules, Sarah. Turn around."

She did, and he toweled off her backside.

"My belt left a couple of welts," he said.

She reached back to feel, and he guided her hand over one. "I like admiring them."

"Sounds very submissive."

"I found that tracing them was contemplative, and it grounded me. I would remember the way you told me you loved me before you ever touched me. I'd recall the sound of your voice and the way you'd take care of me. That kind of tenderness from such a big man always surprised me a bit."

He captured her shoulders and turned her to face him. "You've said you've never experienced anything like we had."

She shook her head. "No."

"I haven't, either. Any of it."

She finished for him, "Including the betrayal."

He pulled the clip from her hair. "Go get on the bed. On all fours."

Wondering what he was thinking, she followed his order.

He walked across the room.

Curious, she turned her head to one side so that she could see what he was doing.

He pulled open a dresser drawer and removed a small dildo-looking thing.

"What is that?"

"A butt plug. You're not the only one who brought toys, gorgeous subbie. I'm going to put it in you, and you're going to wear it all night. If it needs to come out, I'll remove it for you."

Sarah felt the color drain from her face.

"Later tonight you'll be grateful I stretched you out."

"Is it plastic?"

"Glass."

She curled into a ball. "That doesn't sound safe."

"It's safer for you than willful disobedience."

Fighting the urge to tell him to stay ten feet away from her, she got back into position while he stood there, silently regarding her.

"Good." He nodded. He grabbed a bottle of lube and applied several liberal dollops to the toy before approaching her.

"Pretty sure I'm not going to like this," she said.

"Pretty sure I didn't ask."

"Yes, Sir."

"Forehead on the mattress, ass high in the air."

Her body shook as she complied.

"Now reach back and spread your buttocks."

When he'd said he'd test her, he'd obviously meant it. As soon as she'd complied, she felt the tip against her anus. Assailed by nerves, she squirmed away.

"It's up to you how difficult this will be. You can bear down and let it in. Or you can tense up and fight against the intrusion. If you want to make it difficult, I'll indulge you. I'll dunk it in an ice bucket before I put it in you."

His tone was flat and emotionless.

"Either way, Sarah, unless you use your safe word, this plug is going in your ass and it's staying there all night."

He leaned over her and brought his face in close to hers.

His lips were set, his eyes narrowed. The charming, teasing companion was gone, replaced by an intractable Dominant.

"The plug is completely safe. I'd never go anywhere near your body with something that wasn't. You could drop it on a tile floor and it wouldn't break. But before using it, I will always check it for chips."

"Yes, Sir." In spite of what he'd said, her whole body was tense.

"Are we clear?"

"Yes, Sir. That thing is going in my ass."

He feathered hair back from her face. "Please me, sub."

That was all she needed. She nodded. "I'm ready."

He fingered her clit, then teased her pussy. Since he'd aroused her in the tub, it didn't take long for the nerve endings to flare again. He slipped inside her to draw moisture back to her anus.

With the way he teased her, she began to relax.

When he replaced his finger with the rounded glass tip, she tightened her muscles.

"Keep breathing."

It always amazed her what a difference that made.

He pulled away and waited until the tension left her legs.

"You're doing great." He traced a hand up the outside of her left thigh.

His touch reassured her as it always had. It wasn't until she'd played with other men that she'd appreciated Reece's skill.

"I'm ready."

He pressed the plug in a bit farther, and before she could protest, he eased it back out. He gave her no time to think or argue—instead, he overpowered her senses, touching her, kissing her, making soothing noises, playing with her pussy.

Before she could respond to anything, he'd moved on.

As the thicker part of the plug stretched her, she gritted her teeth. "I don't like this."

"You're almost there."

"I really don't like this." The plug was unyielding, nasty.

He pulled it out.

She released her grip on her buttocks.

"Please behave like you're supposed to."

Breathing was easier with that thing a few inches away.

"Sarah."

She responded instantly, parting her ass cheeks, thrusting her hips toward him. "Can we please get it over with?"

Despite her plea, he took his time, fucking her with the plug. After a few strokes, it wasn't as difficult to take. "Put it in," she ordered.

With a laugh, he twisted the hilt and sank it all the way in.

She collapsed onto her stomach. In only a few seconds, her body accommodated the intrusion, her muscle closing around the base. While she was aware of its presence, it wasn't that uncomfortable.

"You're okay?"

"It's not as bad as I thought it would be."

"Most things aren't, once you work them through," he said. "The anus is surprisingly sensitive, an erogenous zone. I figured you'd like it once you stopped fighting it. Fighting me."

She rolled onto her back. *Fighting him.* She'd done that a lot.

"Now, your choice."

He offered a hand to help her sit up, and she took it.

"You can get dressed before I put the choker on you, or I can do it while you're naked."

CHAPTER SIX

"Naked," Sarah said.

Her answer shocked him every bit as much as it delighted him. "Good," he said. "On your knees on the floor."

He helped her from the bed. She only shifted once, presumably because of the plug, before settling. She really had made progress as a submissive. If what she said could be believed, she'd done a lot of it with him in mind.

Reece took the velvet-covered box from the jeweler's bag and opened it near her. "Go ahead and take it out."

She lifted the necklace from the box. "It really is beautiful. Thank you."

"Lift your hair."

While she did, he went behind her and fastened the necklace into place. He held his thumb on the clasp for a moment before asking her to stand. "Come look."

She joined him in front of the mirror.

He stood behind her, hands on her shoulders. "It's perfect on you." He felt inordinately pleased with himself.

Her nipples were hard, and her hair hung in wild, damp disarray. Her stunning green eyes were open wide, and he realized that she was looking at him, not herself. "How are you doing?"

"In this moment?"

He nodded.

"I couldn't be happier."

"For tonight, it's more than a piece of jewelry."

"I understand that. It doesn't change what I just said. I will wear it proudly."

He crossed to the closet and took out the dress that had been delivered.

She let it cascade over her body and settle into place.

"It's even better than I remember," he said. The front V plunged scandalously, and the peekaboo back invited his imagination to run wild. The choker was the perfect accent, bold, eye-catching. He couldn't be more attracted to her than he was at that moment.

"I need to go to my room to do my makeup and fix my hair."

"You look fine, Sarah."

She sighed. "But you have to admit my eyelashes are naked."

"Which is fine with me."

"At the very least, I want a clip for my hair." She glanced down. "And a different pair of shoes."

"Twenty minutes."

"Thirty would be better."

"It wasn't a question."

"Do you always have to have your way?"

"Was that rhetorical?"

"I guess it was." She gathered up her discarded clothing and key card before kissing him on the cheek. "Twenty minutes it is, Sir."

This woman, sub, vixen, was getting to him despite his best intentions.

She left and the door closed with a gentle *snick*.

After shaving, and styling his hair with a dollop of gel, he changed into a pair of slacks, a silk shirt, blazer and tie, along with the bright yellow athletic shoes that had been delivered to his room. Since it would be good for Kennedy's business, Reece slipped them on.

His earlier opinion hadn't changed. They were hideous.

But they *were* like walking on air.

He'd buy another couple of pairs, and turn in an order for several thousand shares of stock.

As she had earlier, Sarah had left her door ajar. He knocked and entered. She'd looked beautiful earlier, but she simply stunned now.

"Turn around," he instructed.

As she did, he gave her a wolf whistle, low, deep and approving.

Her hair was artfully pulled up so that the opening in the back of her dress was more obvious.

Her décolletage had a hint of glitter. It drew attention to the sparkle of her choker, emphasizing it. Her finishing touch, fuck-me red lipstick, made him want to upend her and claim her with his cock. *His*.

"You approve, Sir?"

"You're sensational, Sarah. All of a sudden, I'm considering staying in."

"If you say so, Sir." She smiled.

"I like the compliant side of you."

"I'm very compliant. When I want the same things that you do."

"Have I told you how much I appreciate your honesty?"

She grinned.

"Lift your dress and turn your back to me," he instructed. "Spread your legs, part your ass cheeks, show me that plug."

In that moment, the atmosphere changed. Teasing

vanished. She recognized it, too. With her lips parted, she drew in a deep breath.

"I'm waiting."

"Sir," she whispered, lifting her dress and turning.

Proof of her obedience made raw male pride surge in him. "Ask me to fuck you with it."

She hesitated.

He waited.

"Please," she said. "Fuck my ass with the plug, Reece."

He took hold of the base and pulled out the glass. She grunted, and he slid it back in, using a bit of force to get the fattest part past her sphincter.

She groaned but remained in position.

Confident that she could take it, he fucked her with it, faster and faster.

Her groans became whimpers.

"Talk to me, Sarah."

"It's amazing, Sir."

She was amazing.

He pulled it out and re-seated it a couple of more times. "How does your ass feel?"

"It burns a little."

"So you'll be remembering this for a while?"

"Probably the whole night."

"You can stand up," he said, pushing the plug a bit deeper and causing her to take a tiny step forward.

She shook her head, checked that the clip was still in place then smoothed the dress around her.

"I'll be thinking about your body all night," he told her.

"Tell me you are going to fuck me later?"

"I'm going to hold you down and make you scream."

"Bring it, Sir."

"Brave words."

"It's easy to be brave when you're not in mortal danger."

He caught her chin and captured her gaze. "But you are, Ms Lovett. Most definitely."

She had the good sense to look away.

He released his grip and moved to the door.

"Nice shoes, Reece," she said as she passed him.

"Good thing my slacks are black."

"Sorry to break your heart, but yellow and lime don't go with anything."

"Don't tell Kennedy."

She accepted his arm and they headed to the top-floor restaurant that had a view of the water.

"Sit flat on the plug," he said, even though the hostess was still waiting to hand over the menus.

"Yes, Sir."

He glanced at the wine list and selected a hearty red. "I figured steak tonight. You'll need your strength after issuing that challenge."

"You'll need yours, Sir."

It would be easy to pretend that they'd never been apart, that tonight's party for Julien was like the others they'd attended as a couple, that the future was bright.

After the wine had been delivered, she said, "I'd ask what you're thinking, but I'm not sure I want to know."

"You're right."

The waiter returned to take their order, and she asked for a steak, cooked rare. He never remembered her doing that before.

Minutes later, the server brought a large, pewter salad bowl and tossed the ingredients tableside. "Fresh pepper?" he offered.

Reece looked to Sarah.

She nodded.

"Please," Reece confirmed.

The man filled both plates then, after asking if they

needed anything else, promised to check back shortly.

"I guess that's one of the things about a permanent Dominant/submissive relationship that I find confusing."

Reece put down his fork.

"You sometimes order for me."

"That's a gentlemanly thing, not necessarily a Dominant trait."

"That's not what I'm talking about." She shook her head. "Like last night, with the lobster. Tonight, with the wine."

"Sarah, I trust that you're a grown up. If you want to order for yourself, you're always free to do so. You told me on one of our first dates that you like it when I do it. We were together long enough that I learnt your preferences. And we'd talked about spiny lobster when we were in the Caribbean. But if your tastes have changed, I hope you would let me know. And I trust that if you don't like the wine, you'll order a different bottle. Don't confuse courtesy with me needing to exert my will."

She took a drink of the wine. "You did fine with this."

"Sarah, I always had your best interests at heart."

"It felt… Never mind." She gave a half-smile and took a drink of water. "We agreed not to discuss it."

"Last night you said that I would have consumed you."

"And now I realize it was partially my fault. I assumed things about our relationship that I shouldn't have. I let you take the lead on things where I did have an opinion. We should have talked more than we did." She picked up a crouton. "Did you know I hate these? Fried, crispy, overly seasoned day-old bread that can crack a tooth unless you suck it down to the gluten."

"I had no idea. What else don't I know?"

"That I like to have my feet rubbed. And that I wished I had some nipple jewelry. There, I've shocked you."

"On the contrary. More like fascinated," he corrected. "Are you going to pierce your nipples?"

"I'm not sure about that. But it's a consideration."

He'd never thought of it before, but the idea of leading her around by a delicate chain attached to them...

"I always want more stimulation, and I thought that might help."

"I'm glad you're telling me now. I wish you'd have mentioned it before."

"At that time, it seemed too bold."

"You appear to have the idea that the word Dominant is synonymous with mind reader."

"You always read my body, me, my reactions so well."

"I always paid attention to you. It was my intention that you would never be distressed. But my focus is more on being certain I don't overdo something. It's entirely possible I will miss a signal that you want more of something. Part of the onus is on you to communicate, not only on me to guess."

The waiter returned to clear their plates. There was a neatly stacked pile of croutons next to hers. He scooped them up without saying a word.

"In that case," Sarah said when they were alone. "More nipple play, Sir."

"My pleasure. Would you like to start now?"

"What?"

"Take an ice cube from your water and run it over both nipples."

She folded her hands on the tablecloth. "Are you serious?"

"Do as you're told."

She glanced around, but he'd already ensured that they had privacy before issuing his command.

Her eyes were wide with shock, but they had a gleam of something else, a taste for the forbidden.

She took an ice cube from her glass and let a couple of drops of water drip onto her napkin.

"All your dresses should have that kind of access," he told her.

Sarah trailed her hand down her chest then slipped beneath the fabric. He saw her little winces as the ice chilled her skin, but she sucked in a breath when she touched her nipple.

"Swirl it around." Her obedience, her reaction made his dick stiffen. "Now the other one." Amazing that his voice could sound so commanding and forceful when he felt so aroused.

Like a perfect sub, she did so.

The piece of ice was barely a chip when she dropped it on top of the table.

"Now pull your shoulders back so I can see how hard your nipples are."

She removed the clip and shook out her hair then stretched into an arch.

"Gorgeous, Sarah." Her nipples were erect. Between her seductive smile, the knowledge that his plug was making the position even more uncomfortable for her and the sight of his choker around her neck, he couldn't remember his own name. "I'm tempted to take you back to the room."

"Anything you say, Sir."

He needed to be careful with her. This Sarah could make him do anything she wanted, including forgetting the past.

A few minutes later, the waiter brought out their steaks.

She closed her eyes as she savored the first bite.

"I definitely like the way you show your pleasure."

"You gave me plenty of things to show it about."

After dinner, she ordered key lime pie. And she didn't share.

"We may have to discuss this new-found independent

streak," he told her, fascinated with the way she devoured it, turning the fork over, making sure she caught every bit with her tongue.

In response, she licked the last dollop of fresh whipped cream from her finger.

Shaking his head, he said, "Well, that showed me the evolution of this relationship."

"The evolved Sarah won't be consumed by a Dom. Nor will she let him eat her dessert."

He nodded.

"But she does need to work off some calories."

He stood and offered a hand. "I have an idea or two about that."

She smiled, a cheeky, seductive secret just between them, and said, "I'm counting on it, Sir."

DOZENS OF PEOPLE milled in the lobby, most of them in small groups. Signs pointed the way to the party and even from here, Sarah could hear the sound of a DJ blasting a 1950s dance tune.

Servers passed by with trays of champagne, others canapés. Still others offered obscenely big chocolate-covered strawberries. Reece stopped a woman bearing key lime bites.

"This time, I'm not sharing," he said, popping it into his mouth.

She waited for his reaction. When he raised his eyebrows, she asked, "See why I didn't share? It's kind of like an orgasm for the taste buds."

"I understand." He grabbed a second from the retreating woman.

"Now who needs to work off some calories?" she teased.

"It's a problem we should solve together."

SIERRA CARTWRIGHT

Maybe because of the wine, or perhaps because of their forthright conversations and new-found conviction, or because of the frenetic atmosphere, the fact that she wore a necklace proclaiming she was his, or the butt plug shifting inside her, she had more energy than she'd had in years. It churned inside her, driving her.

The DJ said a few words then the unmistakable sound of an Otis Redding ballad spilled from the ballroom.

"I love that song. Can we dance?" Without waiting for a response, she snagged his wrist and started to lead him toward the dance floor.

"Hold up, Sarah."

She stopped and exhaled.

"Let's try this a different way," he said, leaning down toward her so that she could hear him.

"A different way?"

"I'm still the Dom." His tone sent an illicit thrill down her spine.

"I'm not sure what you mean," she said.

"May I have this dance with my lovely submissive?"

She'd always adored his manners, and the way he managed to seduce her without ever touching her. "Thank you, Sir. Yes."

He placed his fingers in the small of her back. His touch felt possessive and simultaneously reassuring.

At the front of the room, a stage had been erected, and big screens flanked it. Pictures of Julien, his friends, previous parties and, of course, his spacecraft-looking headquarters scrolled past.

Two separate areas with food and beverages had been set up. A tiered fountain was the focal point, and pink bubbly liquid frothed over the layers. No doubt it was filled with the finest sparkling wine available on the planet.

On the dance floor, Reece pulled Sarah against him. "I'll dance with you any time, all night," he said against her ear.

She allowed her body to meld with his.

"I like any excuse to have you in my arms," he said.

She looked up and wrapped her arms around his neck. In this moment, as long as she pretended there was no past and no goodbye looming tomorrow morning, her life couldn't be more perfect.

He moved one hand lower, onto her buttocks. "How's the plug?"

She felt scandalized, even though no one was looking at them. "I can definitely feel it."

He skimmed his fingers lower, between her buttocks, until he felt the glass.

"Sir," she protested.

He pushed on it, and she stood up a little taller.

"I should have insisted on this years ago."

His continual sensuous onslaught was driving her crazy.

The song transitioned to one with a more upbeat tempo.

Reece led her into a two-step. During the time they'd been together, they'd danced often enough that she effortlessly followed him. "You've still got it," she said with a wide grin.

He raised his hand and she spun beneath it before he closed her into a basket move. She grinned when he moved in for a quick kiss.

When the song ended, she said, "You made an excellent choice with this dress. I love it."

The way he looked at her, she knew he was thinking about getting her out of it. Her insides turned molten in response to his sultry look.

They moved over to join Kennedy and a man she vaguely recognized. With their vibrantly colored athletic shoes in an ocean of loafers and wingtips, the two men had captured her attention from across the room.

"He got you into a pair, as well?" Reece commiserated with the unknown man.

"Better than spending the whole night listening to him brag about how comfortable his feet are."

"What do you think of them?" Kennedy asked.

"I'll take stock," Reece replied.

"Why not white or black?" Sarah asked.

"Because they wouldn't be as obvious," Kennedy said. "These make a statement."

"That you're color-blind?" she asked.

"I'll send you some as soon as the women's line is released. You'll be doing my PR for free."

"Right. I'll travel the world and take pictures in various locations. I'll post them on social media."

Reece snagged a glass of bubbly from a nearby server and he raised an eyebrow toward her.

"I'd love one. Thank you, Sir," she said aware that all the men were watching her. Gawking was probably a more accurate word.

"You do know Grant?" Reece asked.

"Actually, I've never met him," she said. "I saw pictures at your house."

"Grant Kingston. Sarah Lovett."

His eyes went wide. After the way she'd been treated by Julien and Kennedy, she should have been prepared for that reaction, but it still stung. Her smile faded. "Pleased to meet you," she said, the words ringing false in her ears. "I've heard a lot about you." That part, at least, was true.

"You as well. Not all of it is good. Does that necklace have any significance?" he asked.

He hadn't offered his hand to shake. She felt as if an Arctic front had dropped down her spine.

Instantly Reece put his hand on her shoulder, in reassurance.

"Forgive him," Kennedy said. "He lives in a cave in New Mexico. Doesn't get out often enough to remember he's supposed to observe social niceties."

"He's only asking what you're wondering," she said. "If the question is, did Reece forgive me and take me back? The answer is no."

Reece tightened his grip. The touch was both reassuring and a warning.

"For the weekend, I claimed this woman," Reece said. "She's mine. She recognizes it, and I have no problem with letting others know it."

"No offense meant," Grant said, raising his drink, something in a highball glass, toward Reece.

"If I were his friend, I'd hate me, too."

"It's not you we dislike," Kennedy answered. "It's just your behavior we question. I'm a bit of an optimist. I wonder if there were extenuating circumstances."

"You should have gone to law school," Reece remarked.

"I think you're on my side, Kennedy." Sarah shot him a grateful smile.

"No one is, really," Kennedy responded. "We give a shit about Reece and want him to be happy."

Her smile faded.

"If you make him happy, fine with me. But I'm looking after my own self-interests." Kennedy shrugged. "I can't afford to keep him in Scotch."

With an entourage worthy of a rock star, Julien walked into the room. He held up a hand, signaling everyone to stop, then he brushed a couple of ladies' hands from his forearm and walked away from the small crowd.

"Purple shoes?" Reece asked when Julien joined them.

"The color of royalty," he said.

"Let me take a picture?" Sarah suggested. She was glad she was no longer the focus of the conversation. To Reece she added, "Buy your stock before we post this photo."

At her direction, they lined up. She took several shots with her cell phone camera before saying, "Okay, ham it up. Show some leg."

"Christ, no," Kennedy protested. "No one will buy my shoes if they see Julien's scrawny legs."

"With all those shoes, I don't even need the flash," she said. From what Reece had said earlier, it wasn't often that the four of them managed to get together, and their shared history made her feel like an outsider.

"Are the shots any good?" Julien asked.

She showed him the pictures, then promised to email them later.

A woman, tall, gorgeous and blonde, joined the group. Her heels were at least three inches, and with her already-impressive height, she was taller than Julien and Kennedy. Her arms were toned in a way that demonstrated she could probably bench press any of the men in attendance.

"Excuse the interruption," she said, with the faintest trace of an accent Sarah had difficulty pinpointing.

Some part of Eastern Europe, maybe.

"You can interrupt anything you want, any time you want," Grant said, stepping to one side. "For any reason."

"You are too kind, Mr Kingston. I do hope you managed some sleep this afternoon."

"Passed out," he said.

To Julien, she said, "The emcee is looking for you, Mr Bonds."

"May I introduce Svetlana Starova," Julien said.

The woman inclined her head. "Delighted," she said, but she didn't make any attempt to meet anyone. "If you'll excuse us, I'll return Mr Bonds to you later."

"She runs a tight ship," Reece observed after Julien and Svetlana had excused themselves.

Kennedy whistled. "Holy hell. It's a wonder you survived, Grant."

"I might have had a cardiomegaly," he said with a goofy grin. "Luckily, in addition to being the world's best pilot, she's also trained in first aid."

Sarah shook her head. How was it that grown, successful men became teenagers again when a beautiful woman showed up?

"You have the same effect on me," Reece told her, as if he'd read her mind.

She leaned into him and savored the way he tightened his grip.

"Especially with that necklace and knowing the plug is moving inside you."

How could his words make her think of nothing but sex?

"How do your nipples feel when the dress moves?"

"A little tender."

"Should one of us offer a toast?" Kennedy suggested.

Grant blanched. "You're welcome to do it."

"You've gotta get out of that cave more," Kennedy said. "Show off your pretty face."

"Svetlana can pry me out."

Before they made a decision, the ballroom lights were turned off.

"Should have figured he'd have it all worked out," Reece said.

"Control freak," Kennedy added.

The gathered crowd hushed. Spotlights hit the stage, illuminating Julien and the emcee, a pop star that even Sarah recognized. The emcee thanked everyone for coming and wished Julien a happy birthday.

SIERRA CARTWRIGHT

"Please join me in singing happy birthday, to a *very* special birthday boy," the starlet invited.

Reece moved Sarah in front of him and wrapped her in his arms. More keenly than ever, she wished that the relationship between them was real.

As the gathered crowd began the song, a cake was wheeled onto the stage. It stood at least six feet tall. On the second mention of the word 'you', the top exploded off and a woman wriggled through the opening, dressed in the blue and white cheerleading outfit of a popular football team. She wore white, knee-high boots and an itty bitty vest with a fringe that drew attention to her bare midriff. She shook her pom-poms in Julien's direction.

The crowd cheered.

As if on cue, another cheerleader bounded up the stairs and onto the stage.

Over the course of the song, it appeared that the entire squad joined in.

"Your rumor was right," she shouted to Reece.

On the big screens, the same cheerleaders could be seen performing a routine in front of Julien's headquarters.

As the song ended, another cake was wheeled onto the stage. The thing was a work of art, and it was designed to look like the first smartphone he'd developed, the one that had made him a multimillionaire before he was twenty-two. Fondant icons with decorative icing represented some of the apps that had been developed for the device. Sparklers on top looked a bit like antennae.

The cheerleaders gathered around him and shook their pom-poms and their asses while he blew out the sparklers.

The pop star led a rendition of *For He's a Jolly Good Fellow* while the cake was removed from the stage.

Julien gave a brief speech, inviting everyone to enjoy themselves and thanking them for sharing the event.

The cheerleaders separated and moved into the crowd as the pop star performed a song that had hit number one in the charts.

"He knows how to entertain," Kennedy said.

"Indeed," Reece agreed. "I find I'm anxious to spend time alone with Sarah," he said. "Kennedy, give me a call the first part of the week. I want to talk to you about investments and Sarah's business."

She exhaled. She'd believed that he hadn't been interested in what she'd had to say earlier. But he'd been listening, like he always had, and thinking.

Over the thundering bass and the singer's reverberating voice, he made their excuses.

"Stairs," he told her.

"We're on the ninth floor," she protested thinking about her heels and the plug.

He linked their hands together and drew her past the bank of elevators and into the stairwell.

On the landing between the first and second floors, he pushed her against the wall.

"I couldn't wait."

His eyes were dark with desire, and lust simmered in his tone.

She couldn't object, wouldn't object. She wanted this man. And she knew time was running out. "Yes," she told him.

Reece plunged a hand inside her dress and closed it around one of her breasts. Her nipple hardened and her knees weakened. "Harder," she told him.

He pinched her nipple until she gritted her teeth.

"Is your pussy getting wet, little sub?"

"My pussy's been wet all night, Sir," she responded.

"Show me."

She lifted her dress.

"I like your bare pussy," he said, sliding his fingers across the smooth skin.

"I like having your fingers there," she admitted.

Before she was ready, he moved his hand up.

The plunging V of the dress's neckline made it possible for him to move the material aside so he could suck on one nipple while he squeezed the other.

She closed her eyes.

His attention was delicious torment. He'd been listening when she'd said how much she liked nipple stimulation.

"I want to be fucked," she said.

He continued to suck as he moved one hand between her legs and plunged his fingers inside her wet cunt.

"Damn, Reece…" She grabbed hold of his head, keeping him close.

He abraded her clit with a fingernail then fucked her pussy with three fingers. The sensation, combined with the pressure from the plug, brought her to the brink of an orgasm. "I'm going to come, Reece."

In response, he bit her nipple.

She screamed, and the sound echoed off the concrete.

Sarah heard a door open, followed by the words, "Everything okay?"

"Svetlana," Reece whispered.

Sarah nodded. "Fine," she called out.

The door closed.

She put back her head and fought to control her racing pulse. Between the fear of being seen and the climax, that wasn't easy.

"Nice to be amongst friends," Reece said. "Now where were we?"

"What?" she demanded. "We should go upstairs."

"We will. But you're going to give me another orgasm first. Cup your breasts and push them together."

She met his gaze.

He gave her a tight nod. For incentive, he began to move his fingers in and out of her pussy.

"We could do this in your room."

"But we are going to do it right here. Hurry. Before we get caught."

The risk added to the tension and the desire. She drew her breasts together.

"Pinch your left nipple."

"It's a little tender from the way you sucked it," she objected.

"Do it."

Keeping her breasts together, she used her thumb and forefinger to squeeze her nipple as he closed his mouth around the other.

This time he finger-fucked her harder, faster than he had before.

She overheated. The way she thrashed her head dislodged the clip, plummeting it toward the concrete. "Hurts," she told him. But she wanted it. "Good."

He sucked harder.

With his fingers, he found her G-spot, and she whimpered.

He continued relentlessly, until her vision blurred.

"Sir? Sir!"

Blood thundered. Then he bit her.

Sarah buried her scream against his jacket, her eyes closed and silent sobs shaking her.

"That's it. That's it."

He cradled her, tucking her under his chin.

Shamelessly, she accepted the support he offered, the same support he'd wanted to spend a lifetime offering her.

"Was that enough nipple stimulation?"

"Is this your subtle way of telling me to be careful what I ask for?"

"Not at all. It was a blatant way of giving you what you want."

"Thank you," she said, looking up and reaching to trace the back of her hand down his cheekbone.

"Now," he said, releasing her and straightening her dress, "let's go back to the room. You can give me a demonstration of downward dog, and I'll throw in an interesting variation."

CHAPTER SEVEN

"Join me for a glass of Scotch?" Reece offered when they were back in his room. Though he enjoyed his friends and the party, he preferred being alone with Sarah. Always had. He liked her company, the intellectual conversation, the fact that at one time, she'd known his business as well as he did.

Earlier, when they'd been talking in the bathtub, he'd had a few ideas about her new business. She was right that there was potential for growth.

She'd said she missed strategizing with him. He'd felt the loss, as well.

Since she'd worked as his assistant, she'd had intimate knowledge of his business. After he'd fired her, she'd taken on a bigger role, that of a confidante and adviser. She knew the players and their personality quirks, and she'd understood how the pieces of his various companies fitted together. Not only that, but she was masterful in social situations.

He could see that she wanted his input, and it was selfish to have withheld it. But offering advice meant they'd be in

SIERRA CARTWRIGHT

touch in the future. Passing her off to Kennedy was a smart decision all round.

Holding up the bottle, he said, "It's Kennedy's finest."

"I'm sure it's fabulous, but I'm not much for hard liquor."

He opened the bottle and grabbed two glasses from the top of the minibar. "This stuff's for sipping."

"You talked me into it. I'll give it a try. Thanks." She crossed to the sliding glass doors. "Sun's setting," she said.

"Want to watch it?"

"I'd love to." She turned back to face him. "Unless you want to get on with it? I'm feeling a little guilty."

"You shouldn't. It's all been about me."

In a gesture he was sure was subconscious, she fingered her choker. "I'm the one who had so many orgasms I can barely stand up."

He splashed two fingers into each glass then carried one to her. "As I said, Sarah, it's been all about me."

She accepted the glass then followed him outside.

He positioned their chairs so they had a great view of the huge ball of fire heading into the ocean, and he made sure that the arms were touching.

"With the mountains, sunsets are very different in Colorado," she said as she curled up in a chair.

"Are you ready to go home?"

"Vacation can't last forever." A good non-answer answer. "You?"

"Three meetings on Monday." Another good non-answer. "And I need to be there for Mom."

"Is everything okay?"

"She asks about you from time to time."

"I liked her. I think you got your affinity for Scotch from her."

"I don't put ice in mine."

"Or in your beer."

166

"Should be against the law." He chuckled. "Anyway, she's had some health challenges, and she broke her hip recently. She's recuperating at home, and she's driving Dad nuts. I go over a couple of times a week to give him a break so he can play a round of golf. I think she appreciates it more than he does."

"Tell her I wish her a speedy recovery."

"She'll like that." He transferred his drink to his left hand and put his right one around her shoulder.

Sounds from the party drifted upwards, drowning the distant roar of the surf.

Sarah took a dainty drink from the glass. "I'd rather it be added to soda or something. Sorry."

"It's a single malt. Finest on the planet." He hid his shudder.

"I tried to warn you. You can drink it if you prefer?"

"I'll get you some soda. As long as you promise not to tell Kennedy."

"Are you kidding me? He barely tolerates me as it is."

Reece went inside and returned with a cola. "How much?"

"Fill up the whole glass. I promise to only corrupt the cheap stuff in future."

"I'd use the word pollute."

She grinned and took a drink. "Much better."

He'd get her ten sodas and ruin an entire bottle of single malt to see her smile like that.

In peace, they watched the sun set.

"I went to our old place to look for you," she said. "I'm not sure where home is to you anymore."

"An apartment downtown. I got tired of the commute."

"How do you like it?"

"It has all the amenities you can think of. Hot tub. Swimming pool. Fitness center." He shrugged. "I don't miss mowing the grass." After she'd left, the house had seemed too big. Lonely. Empty.

"Any regrets?"

"About the house? No." He left the rest unsaid.

The first stars dotted the sky, and the noises from the party grew louder, as if revelers had spilled outside.

Then fireworks exploded, turning the sky green, then orange.

"Oh my God," she said around a gasp. "They're spelling out Julien's name."

"Is that what's going on?"

"He didn't do that at the last party I was at."

"This is a new one."

From below, he heard a chorus of oohs and ahhs.

"I'm hoping you give me something to ooh about."

"How does that plug feel?"

"I'm ready for it to come out," she admitted.

"Stand up."

"Here?"

"Sarah, I'm getting tired of having my orders questioned."

The balcony was enclosed. Anyone looking up might see him standing, but they'd never see her on her knees.

He took the adulterated Scotch from her and put the glass on the railing.

"You're going to tell me that no one has ever actually died from this?"

"Removing a butt plug?"

"No. The humiliation."

"To my knowledge, no. I can promise you, you won't be the first."

She stood. "You want me to take it out here?"

"I'm going to do it for you."

"Oh, hell no."

He looked at her without blinking.

"Wait a minute. You're…ah…serious?"

"I am."

"Are you open to negotiation?"

"What do you think?"

"Could you be?"

He didn't answer.

"I can't believe this. That you're asking for it, or that I'm considering it." Obviously resigned but not happy about it, she sighed. "How do you want to do this?"

"I love watching you contort yourself in yoga positions. Downward dog."

"Downward…"

"Dog."

After only a moment's hesitation, she got into position, palms flat on the floor, index fingers slightly turned out, toes turned under, her rear end high.

He flipped her dress up. "I like looking at you. The plug is stunning. And more, I like that it means you did something to please me, even if it made you uncomfortable."

"Yes, Sir."

"Gorgeous. Made for spanking." He traced a pattern on her buttocks.

She remained quiet.

"Ready?"

"Yes."

First he turned the plug.

"Ugh."

Then he pulled it out with a steady, firm grip. Her ass gaped, and suddenly he couldn't wait to fuck it. "Inside," he said. "Now."

She hurried inside, and he shut the door behind them.

Reece shrugged off his jacket and loosened his tie then went into the bathroom to put the plug on the counter.

"Fetch a condom from the bag. Any color," he called out. "Ribbed or not for your pleasure."

He re-entered the bedroom and she was holding up a flesh-colored packet.

"And lube."

She hesitated then nodded.

"Thank you. Now I want to see you naked," he said when she brought him both items.

Her motions slow, her gaze on him, she pulled off the dress. She tossed it on top of his jacket.

The sight of her, with her bared pussy and gloriously mussed hair, wearing only spiked, heeled sandals and the choker, gave him a full, throbbing erection. "Let's start with you on the bed on all fours."

"I'm nervous."

He heard the slight waver in her voice. He took her shoulders and held her lightly. "Do you need to safe word? Discuss anything?"

"No. Some reassurance, maybe. Like this."

He cradled her face. "I'll be with you the whole time. I'll touch you. Talk to you. But I need you to respond."

She nodded.

He toed off the athletic shoes and kicked them beneath the bed.

"May I?" she asked, reaching for his belt.

"Please." He held up his hands.

Lowering her head, she undid the buckle then opened his top button and his zipper then let the trousers fall to the floor. "All night I was wondering if you had anything under those." She gripped his cock and stroked.

After a few seconds he stopped her. "No. And you won't change my mind by pouting."

"I wasn't going to pout."

"You were going to use any means to influence me."

"Maybe," she admitted.

"And you won't earn a spanking, either, by being a brat. I'm onto you, Ms Lovett."

He reached for the condom package, picked it up and ripped it open. He put the condom on his cockhead. "Finish it," he said.

She rolled it down. Then she cupped his balls and squeezed.

"You shaved," she said.

"Do you like it?"

"I do."

Then, done with conversation, he picked her up and deposited her on the bed. "All fours," he reminded her.

She scrambled up.

"How sore are your nipples?"

"They're okay."

He took a pair of lightweight tweezer clamps out of the duffel bag and placed them on her nipples.

She pursed her lips together for a few seconds, shook her head then said, "Thank you, Sir."

"You'd do well with piercings."

"Except during the healing time," she said.

"Maybe you'd need to have your hands bound for a couple of weeks."

"Depends who's doing the binding, Sir."

He stroked her buttocks then pulled her back toward the edge of the bed. "I'll keep one hand on you at all times," he promised. "Skin-to-skin reassurance."

"Do your worst, Sir."

Unsure whether he'd been insulted or not, he responded, "I'm hoping you'll find it to be my best."

He aroused her pussy with slow, light touches until she began to writhe. Still touching her, he used his free thumb to depress the pump in the lube bottle, squirting the gel onto his fingertips.

She tightened her muscles, but he continued to play with her until she shifted.

"Good," he said. "One finger. Smaller than the plug."

Since she'd been stretched out, his finger went in easily enough. He rotated his finger to make sure she was properly lubricated before easing out. "Not so bad. Now two."

He placed his forefinger and second finger together and entered her.

"That's a little more difficult," she said around a gasp.

He spread his fingers apart. "Bear down."

"Yes, Sir," she whispered.

He continued to play with her pussy. As she swayed, the nipple clamps moved, distracting her, he imagined.

"How's that?"

"Not as bad as I feared."

"Good." He pulled out and surged forward again. "You're doing great."

Aiming to surprise her, he slid his cock in her pussy.

"Definitely nothing to worry about," she said with a laugh.

He fucked her pussy with his cock, her ass with two fingers. He moved faster, and he inserted a third finger.

"I felt that," she protested.

"Can't trick you," he said. He bent to kiss her buttock. "You're doing fine."

"I'm almost ready to come."

"Hold on."

"But…"

Tone harsh to cut through her building delirium, he instructed, "Wait, Sarah." He pulled out his dick and fingers. Keeping his promise, he put his left hand on her back while he slathered gel on the condom.

"Good Lord!" she said when he inserted his cockhead in her ass. Her body went rigid.

"That's the biggest part," he reassured her.

"It doesn't feel anything like the plug."

"Press your chest to the mattress."

While she moved, he took hold of her hips and readjusted her position. "Put one foot on the floor for balance."

"I've never seen anything like this in yoga class."

"Dolphin position?" he suggested.

"Modified. Very modified," she said.

But she was reaching out to him, not freezing or panicking.

"Best looking dolphin I've ever seen," he said. "Bear down." Before she had time to protest, he pulled her back and simultaneously thrust deep in her.

She yelped and tried to pull away.

"You're there." He had her pinned beneath him. "You did it."

"Good. So we're done?"

He bit her near the ribs. "How are you doing?"

"It's strange, a little uncomfortable, but I surprisingly like it."

"You are a constant source of amazement." He lifted some of his weight so she could move a little. He put a finger on her clit then began to pump his hips.

In less than a minute, she started to move with him.

"I think I could orgasm, Sir," she said.

"You earned it. Take it."

She reached back and began to finger her pussy. He moved his hand faster as her breaths came closer together.

"Come for me, Sarah."

Gasping, she climaxed, and the force of her squirming and pushing her hips back made him ejaculate.

Under his force, she collapsed onto the bed. He had one hand trapped beneath her, and he tangled the other one in her hair, feeling the solidness of his choker around her neck.

He continued to hold her until his cock went flaccid. "Shower with me?"

"If I can stand."

"I'll help you."

In the bathroom, he turned on the shower to warm the water then disposed of the condom before entering the stall with her. He soaped her and rinsed her and said nothing as she stood beneath the spray. "Thank you for that, Sarah."

"It was…" She looked up at him. "I'd do it again."

"Highest praise possible."

She allowed him a miserly amount of water, but he didn't complain.

"Stay the night with me?"

"Yes."

They dried off, and he found her a T-shirt to sleep in. She was asleep before he'd turned off the light. He pulled her against him like he used to in the past and probably never would again.

———

Coffee, fresh, hot, strong and wafting beneath her nose…?

Sarah opened one eye. Reece was sitting on the bed next to her, looking ridiculously handsome with damp hair, an unshaven face and dressed in a golf shirt with khaki pants. He'd left the top two buttons undone, showing a smattering of hair that she itched to run her hand through. But the most fabulous sight was the steaming coffee.

"If this is a dream, it's a good one." She opened her other eye and rose onto her elbows.

"How do you feel?"

Sensations bombarded her. A slight sting where he'd fucked her ass, a throbbing where he'd toyed with her pussy, a dull ache in her nipples, maybe a bruise on her right buttock. "Like we had a night of debauchery."

"Good. Otherwise we'd need to start over."

"Oh, in that case… What debauchery? I had a nice dinner, came home, drank some dreadful Scotch, but then fell asleep around eight o'clock and slept all night."

He grinned.

She managed to wriggle into a sitting position and propped her shoulders against the headboard. "That coffee is for me, isn't it? You're not teasing me or using it as a bribe? Because if you are, name your terms and let's get on with it."

"All yours. You don't have to share. I do know how that's an issue for you."

"You're right. It's up there with key lime pie."

He handed it over.

"I was starting to worry that I might need to wrestle you for it."

"I'll settle for watching you participate in a wet T-shirt contest. Size extra small."

"You're starting to enjoy this too much."

"Bare midriff. Like those cheerleaders."

She took the first delicious sip. "Have you been up long?"

"An hour. Had breakfast with Julien."

"How did I sleep through that?"

"I tried to wake you up. There's a text message from me on your phone."

"I didn't know you had my number." The statement was a vicious reminder of the distance between them. Despite everything they'd shared, he hadn't given her his, either. "Wait. Julien gave it to you."

"No. I'm much cleverer and resourceful than that. I sent myself a message from your phone."

"And you got past my password, how?"

"Your birthday. Got it on the first try."

"You remembered?" Then she added, "Don't answer. I'm not responsible for ridiculous questions before I finish my first cup. Obviously, if you got the password, you remembered my birthday." She knew she was babbling, trying to cover her upset about where they were in their relationship. "You did well on this, by the way. Thank you."

"Easy." He pointed at the cup. "Fill to here with cream. Then top off with coffee."

"You're a quick study."

"When the subject matters."

She drew her knees to her chest.

"Which ferry are you taking back?" he asked, another painful reminder that their time was almost over.

"I'd planned to take the first one—that way I don't miss my plane. There's only a couple of non-stops, and I don't want to get back too late. It's a four-hour flight. I still need to get groceries. You know, get ready for the week."

"Reality calls."

Sarah hated the sudden awkwardness after the weekend's intimacy and honesty. It didn't matter that they'd pretended to start over, the reality was—they hadn't. Distrust and betrayal still lay between them.

His phone rang.

"Julien?"

He looked at the screen. "My parents. Excuse me." He answered and wandered outside to the patio.

She sat there, unsure what to do. Lingering served no purpose. In fact, it might make her look desperate.

There were a dozen details she needed to handle, confirming her seating assignment, packing, checking out. And somehow she needed to keep control of her emotions before she said or did something stupid.

He hadn't discussed a future, asked her to stay, even hinted that he'd like to do anything other than fuck her.

What the hell had she expected?

She'd come here hoping that a scene would help her to forget him. Instead, she was even more in love than she'd ever been.

When she'd left two years ago, she'd been sure that her heart was breaking, but that running and hiding was ultimately her only choice. Over the years they'd been apart, she'd told herself that her memory was faulty. There was no way what they'd shared had been that rich, complex, complete.

She'd been wrong. The time together had proven that their relationship had been everything she'd remembered.

Her new-found understanding of what her disappearance had done to him made this parting worse than the first. Back then, she'd been so focused on protecting herself that she hadn't considered how her reactions would devastate him.

Convincing Julien to assist her and planning Reece's seduction had been the biggest mistake of her life. Nothing, nothing had compared to this kind of heartbreak.

Selfishly, when she'd concocted this idea, she hadn't thought through the implications for him. She'd decided what she wanted and had pursued it with the same single-minded determination that she applied to her business goals.

Looking back on the weekend, she realized he'd been kinder than she'd deserved.

If the situation had been reversed, she would have been furious.

In trying to protect his friend, Julien had tried to talk her out of it. If she'd have been smarter, she'd have listened.

Sarah's hand shook, and she slid the cup onto the nightstand before she spilled coffee all over the bed.

He came back into the room, and closed the sliding glass door.

"I think I'll take a shower in my own room since my stuff is there," she said. No need to prolong the parting.

"I need to leave. My mom's in the hospital."

Stark lines were etched next to his blue eyes, and his voice, normally so rich and modulated, cracked. All the years she'd called him the Iceman, she'd been wrong. He was capable of caring deeply.

She swallowed the knot lodged in her throat, aching that she hadn't appreciated him when she'd had the opportunity. "Is there... What can I do to help?"

"Nothing." He shook his head. "Dad called an ambulance. Said she's stable and it's probably nothing. But he figured, rightly, I'd be pissed if he didn't call."

At one time, she'd had the right to be there for him, and part of her wished that was still true.

"Julien's arranged for Svetlana to fly me to Houston."

"I'm glad." She climbed out of the bed. Suddenly she felt self-conscious standing in front of him wearing only one of his T-shirts. She tugged on the hem, more for something to do than really thinking it would help to cover her. "I know you'll feel better once you're on the way."

"Sarah..."

"You need to go." It seemed wrong to strip in front of him, so she grabbed up her dress from the night before and went into the bathroom.

When she came out, wearing a dress that now seemed scandalous, he was standing near the bed, the duffel bag on top of the mattress and a small suitcase sitting next to it.

"We should talk."

She gave a brave smile. "I want..." How could she express everything she felt in only a few words? Taking a breath, she tried again. "This weekend... I'm sorry. It was a mistake."

"No. I'm glad you came."

He crossed to her and put his hands on her shoulders.

Last night, when he'd done that, his grip had reassured. Now she detested it. It implied an intimacy that didn't exist and hadn't for two years.

"I need to give you back your choker."

"Keep it."

"I can't." She shook her head. "It was too expensive."

"I want you to have it."

"Maybe you can sell it online, or maybe return it?"

"Sarah," he warned. "Stop."

"Donate it to charity. Do something good with it."

"Keep it. It looks stunning with that dress." He traced a fingertip along her collarbone.

The idea that he didn't care if she wore it for another man sucked the air from her lungs. His words chilled her all the way to her soul.

While he was capable of expressing love, he reserved his compassion for those who'd proved their loyalty.

"Thank you," she said, simply to end the argument. When she arrived home, she'd take it off, put it in her jewelry box and never look at it again.

Numb, she pulled away from him.

He didn't try to hold on.

"I hope your mom is okay." With tears burning her eyes, she fled without looking back.

CHAPTER EIGHT

"I finished a third consultation with your Sarah," Kennedy said.

Reece pushed away from his desk and stood.

He'd been stuck on the same proposal for over an hour. That never happened.

In a recent business magazine profile, he'd been labeled as a master strategist. That was an exaggeration, but he did have a talent for looking at businesses as a whole, from financials to marketing plans, and knowing what steps they should take next, from pursuing an acquisition, to proposing a merger, to selling, liquidating, or even going public.

The fact that he'd closed his office door and set his desk phone to 'do not disturb' and that he'd been staring at the same fucking file for twenty minutes told him his mind was elsewhere.

"Did you hear me?" Kennedy asked.

"She's not my Sarah."

"Then why am I giving her free business advice?"

He should have had his cell phone on silent, too. When he'd seen Kennedy Aldrich's name on caller identification, he'd been grateful for the interruption. Until he'd realized that Aldrich wanted to talk about the source of Reece's distraction. "Bill me for it."

"So she is yours."

"Fuck you, Aldrich." He paced to the window and stared to the east. On the vast Texas skyline, storm clouds were gathering, matching his bleak mood perfectly. If he'd had the opportunity, he'd have ordered this weather. A pisser of a gray, bleak winter day.

"Do you want to know what advice I'm giving her?"

"No."

"Or how many hours I'm going to bill you for?"

"Just send me the invoice."

"There's a comma in it."

"It better have been damn good advice."

"She's in a good place to make this into a franchise."

"I'm sure you'll put her in touch with the right people. Keep an eye on things."

"It'll cost you," Kennedy warned. "I generally turn these things over to an associate."

"Keep an eye on it."

"You got it."

"Did she send you the picture of all of us wearing our walking-on-air athletic shoes?"

"Surprised it came out with all that blinding color." He didn't want to admit that he hadn't seen it.

"I forwarded it to Julien. He has the no photos rule. But that picture would be a hell of a coup for the product launch. I'm waiting on his decision as to whether we can use it for PR purposes or not."

"Not until you've got me some stock and a way to make certain this conversation doesn't qualify as insider trading."

They exchanged pleasantries, and they agreed to meet in

Las Vegas at the big tech show hosted each spring by Julien's company.

"How's your mom?"

"Good, thanks. Once they got her blood pressure regulated, they sent her home. Wasn't a heart attack."

"That's a relief. Jacqueline and Thomas send their regards." As if to keep them at a distance, Kennedy referred to his parents by their first names.

"I'll be sure to tell her, thanks."

"And your dad's golf game?"

"He says you won't stand a chance next time the two of you play. He wants to know if you're still being a pansy and riding in a cart."

"Ouch."

"And the answer is?"

"I thought a pansy was a flower."

"Is it?" If it wasn't for the service that came in and watered and pruned his foliage once a week, he'd have nothing alive at his apartment.

"Anyway, yeah, I still ride a cart. I get to the clubhouse quicker that way."

"Then why play golf?"

"I don't. Hate the sport. I swing at a ball as an excuse to drink before noon and ride around with people I'm going to take money from. More deals are made on the golf course than in any boardroom."

Reece shook his head.

"You doing okay?"

"If the question is do you need to send Scotch? The answer is no."

"Wasn't worried. Got a charity event in DC this weekend. Could use the moral support."

He'd seen the invitation. "And a check for ten thousand dollars for a platinum-level sponsorship?"

"Not necessary. Thought you might want to help me with some of those debutantes Jacqueline keeps shoving at me."

"I'll send a check."

"I was afraid of that."

"Poor you. Your choice of a dozen beautiful young women."

"With dreams of babies and access to my bank account."

He didn't envy his friend.

"For the record, McRae?"

"Yeah?"

"Sarah doesn't sound any better than you do."

"I didn't ask."

"You didn't have to."

Kennedy ended the call.

Reece turned and tossed his phone onto the desk. He knew the screen wouldn't break, thanks to the impermeable box that surrounded it. Another of Julien's minor inventions.

He paced the office until he realized he was accomplishing nothing. Nor had he for the past two weeks.

For the first few days he'd been back in Houston, it had been relatively easy not to think of her. He'd been busy helping his dad and caring for his mother while juggling his work responsibilities.

Then, when Georgia had started to feel better, he'd slept for almost twenty-four hours.

He'd woken with a hard-on and Sarah on his mind.

Frustrated, he'd taken a shower and jacked off. But as he'd closed his eyes, he'd imagined fucking her hot, tight cunt.

Even though his ejaculate had spurted onto the tile floor, it hadn't got rid of the churning in his gut.

It was then that he'd realized he couldn't pretend the island weekend hadn't happened.

For the next week, he shoved aside thoughts of her.

He'd driven himself to work sixteen-hour days. After work, he had hit the gym, relentlessly pushing himself until he reached exhaustion. With everything he had, he'd willed time to pass.

That had been the only thing that had saved him two years ago when she'd vanished. It would be the only thing that helped this time.

Now that Kennedy had brought her up, there was no avoiding her.

So what if she wasn't doing well?

And what the hell did that mean, anyway?

He strode to his computer, backed up his file, grabbed his keys and cell phone then crossed into the reception area. "I'm taking the rest of the day off," he told Karen.

"Everything okay, Mr McRae? Any special instructions?"

Generally she patched calls through to his cellular when he was out of the office. "Take messages."

"Will you be back in tomorrow?"

"I'll let you know."

At his apartment building, he hit the fitness center and did almost an hour on the rowing machine, until his arms ached and his lungs burned.

The exercise didn't banish the memory of her.

After wrapping a towel around his neck, he jogged up the eight flights of stairs to his apartment.

Despite the fact that it was only mid-afternoon, gloom sucked the color from the walls. Thick, slushy drops of rain pelted the bank of windows and wind shook the panes in their casings. He closed the blinds and turned on the over-head lights.

Reece flipped the switch to ignite the living room fire-place. When he'd first moved in, the gas-burning logs had seemed like an unnecessary addition, but he'd learned to welcome its presence on dreary, cool days like today.

He grabbed a bottle of water from the kitchen before heading into the master bedroom.

Near the dresser, he paused.

Her original collar still lay at the bottom of a drawer. Why he'd kept it, he couldn't explain. It had been ordered for her, but throwing away something so expensive had seemed ridiculous. Briefly, he'd considered selling it. But setting up an account at an online auction house to sell one item seemed like a waste of time. And he hadn't wanted to take it to a jeweler. Most of all, he hadn't wanted to imagine it around the neck of another sub. Even to himself, that rationale seemed shaky. He should have got rid of it.

And he sure as hell shouldn't be thinking about looking at it right now.

But he was.

Even though there were a dozen good reasons he shouldn't, Reece opened the drawer and removed the red velvet pouch.

He loosened the drawstring and pulled out the collar.

The years had taken some of the luster from the metal. He grabbed a T-shirt and ran it over the surface until the over-head light danced its reflection off the silver.

She'd been right when she'd told him the metal was thick. He'd ordered it that way. The three millimeter width was intended to make a proud, unabashed statement about her, about them.

But he hadn't meant it to intimidate her.

Looking at it now, critically, he could see why she'd been scared.

Wearing it would require a lot of confidence. The whole world would know about their relationship. And she might be asked questions. She was right that people outside the life-style would be curious. This collar wasn't subtle like the choker, something that could be passed off as a beautiful accessory.

Words Kennedy had spoken on the island returned to haunt him. *There's a difference between real fear and being a coward.*

In his greed to make his claim on his woman, he hadn't been as aware of her needs as he'd thought. Blithely, he'd believed that everything was okay, that she was as comfortable as he was, that their relationship was progressing to the point where she'd want to be married and collared. The realization that they'd never discussed what that would mean to each of them stunned him.

Despite that, she'd sought him out. She couldn't have known what reaction she'd get from him. But she might have guessed that he'd still be angry and would demand that she atone for the sin of leaving him. He'd told her he'd test her, and she'd met his every challenge, physical and mental. She'd even valiantly accepted a choker that represented his collar. As he looked back, it humbled him.

All along, he'd blamed her without looking to himself as the reason for her fear. Because of what he'd needed from their relationship, it had been his responsibility to keep those lines of communication open.

The knowledge that he'd failed her shook him.

For one of the first times in his life, he was unsure of his next step.

How the hell did he make amends when he'd fucked up beyond redemption? He recalled the stark hurt on her face, her brave smile, the sheen of tears covering her big green eyes before she'd fled from his hotel room.

How could he have been stupid enough to let a woman that beautiful, that courageous walk out of the door?

Fuck.

He picked up his phone and dialed the Genius of the Known Universe.

"How'd the grand adventure go?"

Sarah put down her latte and looked at Loretta. Her long-time client had become a friend, and it had been her words that had inspired her to contact Julien to arrange the meeting with Reece. "The party was great," Sarah responded, evaded. "Julien can throw himself a hell of a party."

"That's not what I'm asking. You know it."

Sunlight dappled through the downtown Golden coffee shop window. Today was one of the reasons she liked Colorado in the winter. The sky was brilliant blue. The recent snow had melted, and a promise of spring whispered on the chinook wind.

To escape her own thoughts, she'd called Loretta, slapped on a helmet, grabbed her bike and a credit card then ridden ten miles before ending up here. The endorphins helped the burn in her muscles, but not the ache in her heart. "I haven't heard from Reece since I got back."

"So you did see him at the party like you were hoping?"

"He was there."

"And?" Loretta prompted. "Do I need to get a crowbar to get answers out of you? Give it up."

How to explain what had happened? The fabulous, boundary-pushing sex, the sensual feel of his leather lash, the seamless way they'd danced together, the off-the-hook sex in the stairwell, the dinner spanking, the connection, the intimacy, the teasing.

"Or did you discover that he wasn't as fabulous as you remembered? He'd got old and fat."

"He's handsome as ever."

"I know. I did an Internet search. Does his personality match? He seemed to have a nice smile, but I wasn't sure if it was forced. I know you call him the Iceman."

"Emotionally, toward me, he still is. But…" She trailed off.

"You had sex?"

She nodded.

"Was it good sex?"

"At least passable." Sarah laughed. She should have expected the question. She and Loretta shared a lot of secrets. Even though the woman looked prim and proper with her coiffed hair, pencil-slim skirt, figure-shaping stockings, sensible pumps and a strand of pearls resting on her blouse, she had a twisted sense of humor. She went to the comedy club with friends at least once a month, and the raunchier the comedian, the more she enjoyed it. "Yeah. It was better than I remembered."

"Anal?"

"Loretta!" She glanced around the coffee shop.

"And he brought out whips and chains, didn't he?"

Sarah collapsed against the back of her chair. "Is anything sacred with you?"

"Are you kidding me? I'm living vicariously through you. I want every single detail." She took a bite of biscotti and waited.

"Yes."

"Yes to what?"

"Yes to all of it."

"No!"

"Yes."

Loretta dropped her biscotti into her cup. *"All* of it?"

"All of it."

"So what the hell is wrong with your young man?"

"There's nothing wrong with him."

"Is he gay?"

189

"What? No." Sarah laughed.

"Is he married?"

Sarah shook her head.

"Engaged?"

Again she shook her head.

"Committed to some other woman?"

"Not to my knowledge."

"Then something is wrong with him," Loretta claimed. Using a spoon, she fished the swollen biscuit from the bottom of her cup. "If he let you come back to Colorado alone, there's something wrong with his head."

"He's not going to forgive me. I took your advice. And I tried."

"Do you love him, still? Or did you find out that it wasn't as good as you remembered?"

Sarah thought about that. "It was better." They'd communicated better than they had before. They'd spoken honestly, openly. He'd been everything she'd hoped, kind, considerate, mannerly, possessive.

"Then call him. Tell him to lace up his big boy shoes and come and claim you."

Sarah grinned at that thought. Call up a Dom who'd made it clear that he didn't want her and boss him around. "I'll get back to you on that."

"Mark my words, young woman."

She picked up her latte. "You told me I owed it to myself to find out. You were right. Somehow, I just have to quit thinking about him." Obsessing was more like it. She went to sleep with him on her mind, dreamed of him then woke up thinking about him only to spend the whole day trying to ignore those thoughts.

Every once in a while, she looked at the pictures she'd taken of the four guys at Julien's party. If she were smart, she'd delete them.

But when it came to Reece, smart was a vague concept.

"I'm thinking about starting a new business, an event dating site," Loretta said. "Ten people, five women, five men, five day catamaran cruise."

Already thinking of a marketing campaign and splashy ideas for a website, Sarah nodded.

"I think you should be my first client. Get back on the horse."

"That's a mixed metaphor. Get back on the horse, but the horse is really a boat."

"Sail into the sunset with a new man?" Loretta suggested.

"I wish it were that easy." Sometimes it seemed the harder she tried to forget him, the more pervasive his memory became.

"Then give me his phone number, and I'll call him."

"I believe you would."

"Man's an idiot to let you go. He needs to be slapped upside the head. I'm happy to do it."

"Honestly, Loretta, I don't want a man who I have to convince."

"Well, that might not be a problem. Might want to put down your drink."

Frowning, she did.

"Let me know how it goes." Loretta picked up her designer leather purse and said, "Thanks for the coffee."

"That's it? You're leaving?"

"I'll get back to you on the dating site idea." She stood.

Then Sarah heard, "Is this seat taken?"

Her heart stopped.

Stunned, she turned around.

Reece?

"Reece McRae?" Loretta asked. "Saw your picture online. Treat this woman well, young man, otherwise you'll deal with me," Loretta said, pointing a finger at him.

"I will, ma'am."

Loretta winked and said goodbye with a quick wave.

Reece slid into the vacant seat across from her.

He looked…amazing. His dove-gray suit was tailored and made his hair seem even darker by contrast. His red tie radiated power. His crisp shirt invited her to crease it.

A hundred questions slammed together in her mind, and she couldn't sort out a single one, so she stared, her pulse in overdrive, her stomach a twisted knot.

"I fucked up."

She opened her mouth then closed it again. "Welcome to Colorado," she said because she couldn't think of anything else.

"GPS coordinates," he said. "From your phone number."

"What?"

"You're wondering how I found you. Genius of the Known Universe figured he'd save me some time, so he texted me with your location."

"Handy."

"He wants his plane back."

"I'm trying, Reece. Really, really trying to figure out what's going on here." She couldn't dare allow herself to hope.

"Are you finished with your coffee?"

She nodded.

"Let's go to your place."

"I rode my bike." Which meant that she was hot, sweaty and had helmet hair. She didn't look a thing like she did in her fantasies. "I can meet you at the house. Better yet…" She finger-combed her hair. "I can meet you later for dinner. After I've cleaned up." Someplace neutral, where he wouldn't dominate the space.

"I have an SUV."

"A nice one," she said when they went outside.

"Helps to know a genius."

He loaded her bicycle then helped her into the passenger seat before climbing behind the driver's wheel and merging into traffic.

"Let me guess, you don't need my address."

"Helps—"

"To know a genius," she finished for him.

Figuring that she wouldn't get much more out of him until he was ready, she settled back and tried to practice some yogic breathing. She failed. Her breaths were closer to shallow gasps.

This close, his windswept scent enveloped her, comforting and unnerving her at the same time.

A lock of dark hair had fallen across his brow, but it softened the scowl buried there.

He navigated to her complex and parked in a visitor's slot.

She didn't protest when he unloaded her bike and carried it up the stairs to her front door. A long time ago, she'd learnt not to fight him when he was this quiet and focused.

"If you prefer dinner," he said, "I'll come back for you in an hour."

"No. This is fine. You've seen me at my worst."

Inside, after she'd closed and locked the door, she took off her bicycle shoes. He was so much bigger than she was. When she was in a scene or when she was in heels, she didn't notice it as much. Now, adrenaline flooded her in little bursts that kept pace with her heartbeat.

"Nice place," he observed, wiping his wingtips on the mat.

"Can I offer you something to drink?" she asked. She headed toward the kitchen. Acting like a hostess gave her something to do, and she desperately needed that to quell the building agitation. "I'm sorry that I don't have any single malt Scotch," she said over her shoulder, "but there's probably a cheap bottle of red wine or maybe a beer left over from my holiday party."

"Nothing, thanks."

She reached for the refrigerator handle. "Don't mind if I do?"

"I'd prefer you didn't."

His words stopped her.

After dropping her hand, she turned to face him.

"I'd like to talk. And I don't want any distractions." He took out his cell phone and turned it off.

"This seems serious."

"I got strapped in by Svetlana, got hauled across the country at a speed I was sure was going to create a sonic boom and I'm now in debt to Julien Bonds."

"This is serious," she said. "Uhm…" *Unless...* She leaned her shoulders against the refrigerator door and swallowed. In the past, she'd prided herself on reading his moods, and she knew he was agitated, but wasn't sure why. "Is your mom all right?"

"Fine. Getting better."

She let out a relieved breath.

"She's hoping I'll come to my senses and bring you home."

"I…" She opened her mouth then closed it again.

"Actually, Dad is, too."

"Reece, please." Being apart was torture enough. But the idea that he'd talked about her to his parents? It wasn't fair to give them false hope. They loved their only son, and she knew they desperately wanted to see him happy. "Please don't say things like that to me."

He plowed his hand into his hair, and she realized that was why the lock had fallen across his forehead. Reece looked as nervous as she felt.

"May I?" He indicated one of the bar stools in front of her granite countertop.

"Please. Can I take your jacket?"

"No. Thanks."

So he wasn't planning on staying.

"You're brave," he said as he sat.

"I'm brave?" She scoffed. "I was trying to imagine what you might have to say, what brought you here. But that didn't make the list." Suddenly, she couldn't wait anymore. "Why are you here?"

"To apologize."

"For what?"

"The way I treated you."

"You have nothing to be sorry for. When I look back, I realize that you couldn't have treated me any better than you did. I showed up unexpectedly and I asked you to forget the past, the hurt, the damage. I'm lucky you didn't call me all sorts of names or walk out on me. I should have left the past alone. I'm the one who owes you an apology."

"Kennedy told me there was a line between cowardice and real fear."

"He's right. There is." She wrapped her arms around her middle. "I crossed it."

"No. I misunderstood where it was. When I think about you two years ago, frightened, alone, nervous, I don't blame you for your reaction."

"I should have talked to you. You'd always insisted that we have open, honest discussion. But when the stakes were that high, I couldn't." She pushed away from the fridge, but then, not knowing what else to do, she paced to the far end of the kitchen, putting as much distance between them as possible. "If it were to happen today…"

"Go on."

"That's not fair." She shook her head. "That's too easy. I have the benefit of hindsight, of having evolved into someone I wasn't, someone more capable and sure."

"All things being equal," he said. "Hypothetically, you're now living in Houston."

"Okay."

"And you run a successful franchise operation."

"I like the way you think." Despite herself, her nerves, she smiled. She slipped out of the fantasy world he had been creating. "You've been talking to Kennedy."

He inclined his head.

"I think the man's an optimist," she said. "But thank you for having him call. You didn't need to do that."

"Man's got an eye for what works. If he didn't think this could franchise, he wouldn't have put you in touch with the Blancharde Group. He doesn't spend a lot of time unless he's going to get a good return on investment."

"At any rate, if you hadn't recommended me, I wouldn't have gotten past his switchboard."

"You're probably right. You're welcome."

"So, back to all things being equal?"

"You come home from work, you find a collar in my drawer. It's huge. It's a monstrosity."

"I panic. I freak out. I do the happy jig."

"Want to demonstrate? You wearing a bra?"

"You really are a teenager at heart." There it was, the easy intimacy that had so often defined their relationship. This was what she'd never found with anyone else.

"Are you?"

"Pervert." She exhaled. "I was riding a bike. I'm wearing a jersey and a sports bra beneath it. The girls aren't moving no matter what I do."

"Not sure I can get past the jig, regardless," he confessed. He turned over his cell phone several times.

Outside, a horn honked, and it jolted her. She continued, "But maybe I take out the collar while you're not home and try it on."

He sat up a little straighter.

"Maybe I imagine what it would be like to wear it in public. Maybe I wonder what it means to you. Maybe I call you up and ask what the hell you were thinking. Maybe I take a picture of it with my cell phone and send it to you and ask what the hell you were thinking. Maybe I put it on and kneel in the entryway…" Of the house they no longer shared. After worrying her upper lip, she went on. "Naked, waiting for you to come home."

"Jesus, Sarah."

The atmosphere seemed to thicken and churn. He was picturing it as surely as she was. Did the image make him as hungry as it made her? "Maybe I decide to wait until you mention it. And maybe you do, bluntly one night, telling me to lift my hair because you're damn well going to collar me. Or maybe you talk about it in vague terms over time until I get accustomed to the idea and it no longer seems threatening. Maybe you come home and ask me to fetch it so you can show it to me."

"What would happen then?"

"That sets up another series of choices." Things between them had always worked well when they'd hung in there, talking, even when it was uncomfortable. Especially when it was uncomfortable.

As they talked through the hypothetical, she relaxed, breathed. "I could use the word yellow. Or say cream pie. Or I could tell you to fuck off."

"That's blunt."

"I warned you that the new Sarah won't be consumed."

"Fuck off, it is."

"Or I could tell you that I needed to talk first."

"That sounds downright friendly after fuck off."

She grinned. Warming to her subject, really sorting through it in her mind, she continued, "I could have refused to wear it. That might have caused some damage, posed some risk, but it was an option. My option." She paused. "One thing I now know with certainty? You would have never put it on me without my permission, without us having an agreement as to what it meant. But the bottom line, Reece? I tell my clients when an emergency happens that they can respond or they can react. I reacted, from raw instinct, from fear. Fight or flight was triggered in my brain, and I ran. I'm not proud of it. I've never stopped regretting it."

"You came to Florida, dragged Julien into an elaborate scheme to exorcise the past."

She lifted her hands then let them fall to her sides.

"Did it work?" he asked.

"No." Then, because she had nothing left to lose, she said, "It made it worse."

"How so?"

She swallowed. "I've laid my heart bare to you, Reece. What do you want now? To eviscerate my soul?" *Damn it.*

"Hang in there with me. How are things worse?"

"I realized I still care. You're better than I remembered. Just as kind. Just as implacable." She put her hands behind her on the countertop and pushed forward a little. "The sex is as good as it ever was. And the glimpses of intimacy only showed me what I could have had if I had been stronger."

He nodded.

"My choice destroyed trust."

"And my reactions can leave it that way or take the first steps toward repairing it."

Her body temperature dropped several degrees. "I don't understand."

"I tested you. Again and again. You passed every one of them, and still it wasn't enough."

"It could never have been enough."

"I told myself that. Like you said that night at dinner, things look different when you wear the other person's shoes. You told me not to wear yours. But my mother shoved me right into them."

"She knows?"

"Enough. No real details. She thinks you freaked out when you saw the engagement ring, and if it's okay with you, we'll leave it at that."

"What would you have told them if they saw the collar you got me?"

"As little as they needed to know. You're right about that collar. It's a statement."

"With an exclamation mark," she said.

"It's probably not something you'd want to wear all the time."

She sought his gaze but couldn't decipher anything. "Are we still talking hypothetically here?"

"No."

Her stomach plummeted.

"Maybe I was too rigid."

With the way blood buzzed in her ears, she could barely make out what he was saying.

"That's what my mother helped me to understand. And I didn't like standing in your shoes. I did have expectations. All along, I should have been paying closer attention to you, making sure we were on the same path. I'm a few years older than you are. I was probably more ready to get married than you were. And because it was my idea, I pursued it with the same attention I bring to everything else that I want. It might have seemed too fast for you. But the point is, I never asked." He took a breath. "But I'm asking now."

"I don't understand. What are you asking?"

"Would you come here?"

"I need to stay right here," she said. The risk to her

emotional stability was too great to take a step toward him. If he'd come here to apologize and nothing more, she needed the distance so that she could regroup, smile, wish him well before she showed him out and shattered.

"What do you want, Sarah?"

"Not to take this risk."

"You trusted me with your body, your heart as recently as a month ago. Just one more step."

She wondered if she was strong enough to survive him. "This is the most difficult thing you've ever asked me to do."

"I know. I told you I would test you. I want everything you have to offer, all your fears, doubts, tears."

She shook.

"Give them to me, Sarah."

"I want what I hope you're offering. A second chance."

"I want more than that. I want your total unfettered commitment to us. I want you to keep talking, even if you think I'm not listening. To keep trying as hard as I will. To tell me when things become too difficult for you. Tell me yellow if you need to, even if we're not in a scene. That's what I want from you."

"And in return?" she asked.

"That's my girl." He brought up his chin and met her gaze with steady conviction. "I offer you my devotion. My love. My unfettered commitment to us. My vow that I will put you first. My promise that I will pay more attention to your fears and seek you out before you run." He took a step toward her. "And more? My pledge that I will never again test you the way I did today. I give you my trust."

She took a step toward him.

"The rest we can sort out. The marriage, if you'll have me, and when you're ready for it. You moving back in. The collar I hope you will someday accept, on mutual terms."

She threw herself at him. He caught her up, spun her around.

"I can't live without you, Sarah."

"I don't want to live without you, Reece."

He kissed her, long, hard, deep.

"I love you, Sarah."

She reached up. Fingers trembling, she moved aside the lock of hair that had fallen across his brow. "I love you, Reece. I will marry you. And I'd be honored to wear your collar."

He kissed her again. "I have something else I need to tell you."

She held her breath.

"I'm still hung up on that jig image."

"Come take a shower with me. I'll show you the happy jig."

EPILOGUE

Determination and nervousness colliding inside her, Sarah went to Reece's dresser and took out the red velvet pouch.

She still heard the water running in the shower and he was singing, badly—his college fight song, or something similar. In the two months they'd been living together, she'd learnt his routines. Twenty seconds after he finished the final verse, the shower would turn off. He'd open the glass door, grab a towel from the rack then duck back inside the stall to dry his hair and take a cursory swipe at the rest of his body. He'd wrap the cotton material around his waist then exit. After combing his hair, he'd come looking for her.

She found it, him, his idiosyncrasies charming.

Before she could change her mind and decide to do it later, after the celebratory dinner he'd arranged to commemorate signing a franchising agreement with the Blancharde Group, she placed the pouch on their white bedspread, next to the black dress he'd bought her in the Keys.

She realized that she could no longer hear him singing. Seconds later, silence followed. Her pulse tapped out a thunderous tattoo.

"You almost ready?" he called out.

"I am," she said. "But not in the way you mean."

"Can't hear you. Give me a minute."

Feeling certain she was doing the right thing, but still ridiculously nervous, she knelt, knees spread, hands resting on her thighs.

When he walked out of the bathroom and into their bedroom, he missed a step.

"Sarah…" He froze. "Look at me."

The sight of her gorgeous man, dark hair dripping wet, beads of water clinging to his sexy, toned body, a towel wrapped around his waist, his eyebrows drawn together, took her breath away.

Two months ago, Reece had said that he would never test her again, and he'd been true to his word. He'd been patient, steady and, on numerous occasions, they'd spoken hypothetically about marriage and her collaring. They'd discussed what the commitment would mean to each of them, and a few weeks ago, he'd started writing down their agreement. He'd periodically leave it on the kitchen counter next to the coffee pot, along with a pen for her to make notes or cross things out. Each time they talked or wrote things down, her confidence went up and her fear faded.

He hadn't pressured her to sell her town home, but last week, she'd contacted a real estate agent and had made the listing official. After she'd told Reece, he'd bought her a bird of paradise plant to thank her.

"My God, you're beautiful."

"I…" She lifted one hand then dropped it. "Thank you, Sir."

"Tell me…" He glanced from her to the red pouch, to the dress then back at her again. He curled a hand into a fist at his side. "Tell me this means what I think it does."

"It means that I'm being bold. I'm not sure what the

etiquette book says about this, but I didn't know how to ask and…" She paused, wishing he'd take the lead, make this easier. But now, with the way he stood there, implacable, she knew he'd been waiting for her. "I'm asking, Sir. I'm asking you to put the collar on me before we go out tonight."

"Why?"

"I want to make a statement to you," she said, fighting the urge to whisper. "To me. To the world. I'm yours, your submissive, your partner."

"You've humbled me, Sarah." He crossed to the bed and picked up the pouch. "I want us to be clear—this isn't a permanent collar. We'll shop for one together that you feel comfortable with, or we can put a permanent closure on the choker I bought you at Julien's party. I want, with your permission, to do a more permanent collaring. It can be private if you choose, but I'd like us to exchange vows."

"Yes," she said. That had been on his agreements list, and she hadn't crossed it out.

He shook out the collar.

It was every bit as thick as she remembered, but it was significantly more beautiful. Light danced across the silver surface, and the O-ring looked like a promise, not a threat.

"You're certain?"

"I am, Sir."

He used the hex key to open the clasp.

"Come to the mirror with me. I want to be able to watch your reactions, and I want you to see my reaction when I have it locked on you."

She should have known to expect that he would do this in his unique way. She stood and joined him in front of the cheval mirror.

"Lift your hair."

Their gazes met and held. Intensity radiated from his

eyes, his body. She'd hoped that this would mean something to him. Until now, she'd had no idea how much.

"You have never been more perfect to me than you are in this moment." His words shook, as if raw emotion vibrated across his vocal cords.

He placed the collar around her neck and slid the clasp together.

She sucked in a tiny breath.

Then he locked it and tossed the hex tool onto the dresser. "I love you, Sarah. I thank you. I will always cherish your commitment to us."

The metal lay heavily on her collarbone. She traced a forefinger around the O-ring. The collar was as unyielding as she'd suspected it would be, but the satisfaction in his nod liberated her in a way she could never have imagined.

He turned her to face him. Then with a passion he'd never before shown, he kissed her, consuming but also feeding her fire. He tasted intoxicating, of restrained power.

Part of her couldn't understand why she'd waited so long, but she also had an inner peace that her timing was perfect. They'd redefined their relationship, and she'd honed the skill of directly asking for what she needed.

When he ended the kiss, he scooped her from the floor. "Your first act as my submissive, Sarah?"

"Sir?"

"Move our dinner reservations back an hour."

She grinned. "I was presumptuous, Sir. I already did."

He gazed at her, and it was all she could do not to squirm in his arms.

"In that case, shall we get on with it?"

"Your, ah, rattan cane is next to your nightstand, Sir."

He placed her on the bed and hooked his forefinger in the O-ring. "You are feeling brave."

She'd learnt to tolerate it, but more, in the last few weeks, she'd also started to enjoy its uncompromising bite. There were times it soothed more than others.

"How many strokes, my Sarah?"

"Ten, Sir."

"Ten?"

"It spells out I love you. And I remembered to count the spaces."

"You're perfect, Sarah. Perfect." He sat on the bed. "Have I told you how much I love *you?*"

"Not in the last half hour, Sir."

"In that case…"

At his whispered words, a promised threat, an illicit thrill jolted her. And when he pulled her over his knee, her pussy turned molten.

He snatched up the rigid rattan and said, "Let me spell it out for you."

◊ ◊ ◊ ◊ ◊

Thank you for reading Crave. I hope you fell in love with Reece and Sarah like I did. To be honest, it's one of my favorite stories ever. Some of the inspiration for this book came from my real-life experiences.

The Bonds trilogy continues with Claim.

He won't be satisfied until he claims her.

BILLIONAIRE KENNEDY ALDRICH dodges any romantic entanglement that will lead to marriage. That is until he first sees the stunning beauty, Mackenzie Farrell.

Mackenzie is overwhelmed by Kennedy's attentions. A failed marriage taught her to distrust men, and she's vowed never to walk down the aisle again. It takes all her resolve to resist the devilishly handsome tycoon, and every feminine instinct warns that this man will demand more than she can offer.

Her strength and independence enchant him. For the first time ever, he has met a woman who captures his interest on every level. He intends to claim her, no matter the cost, and prove to her that this time love is worth the risk.

DISCOVER CLAIM

SIGN UP FOR SIERRA CARTWRIGHT'S NEWSLETTER for all the news and exclusive bonus reads.

And I'm happy to offer you a sneak peek at Command, the bestselling conclusion to the Bonds trilogy…

"Sierra Cartwright's writing continues to blow me away." ~Shayna Renee's Spicy Reads

COMMAND EXCERPT

All of Grant's expectations fractured, as if they were an icicle that slammed onto the concrete.

When he'd thought of her as a runaway bride who didn't like the cold, he'd mentally prepared himself for someone nervous-looking, maybe huddled in a parka, curled up into herself.

Instead...

Instead, this woman had her shoulders back and held her spine regally straight. And she looked down at him as if she owned the planet.

Wind whipped her brunette hair around her face. She wore a tight-fitting black jacket, an indecently short skirt, tights, and spiked-heel boots that went up and up until they disappeared under her hem.

She was temptation and sin wrapped in a tall, fuckable package.

Every male instinct in him flared, and Grant almost tripped over his own libido.

The man leaning against the side of a nearby SUV stunned Aria. *Grant Kingston.*

A supple brown leather bomber jacket snuggled his upper body. His jeans were a slightly faded shade of blue, and he wore motorcycle boots. The wind tossed a dark blond lock of hair over his forehead.

As he pushed away from the vehicle and strode toward the plane, he pulled off his sunglasses and placed them on top of his head.

His approach was purposeful.

She adjusted the duffel bag on her shoulder and tightened her grip on her briefcase before descending the stair's planes to the tarmac. She told herself her legs were bit wobbly from sitting next to Svetlana—the pilot—and seeing, up close, how challenging the landing was with the airport's infamous crosswinds. But the truth was, the idea of being in intimate proximity with a man this good-looking for any length of time unnerved her.

After she'd returned home last night, she'd spent an hour online looking up stories about him. For someone who was such a prominent part of the Bonds conglomerate, there were surprisingly few.

He'd received requisite mentions in the business and tech sections, but she saw the same photographs many times, which likely meant the news sources all used the same stock photos.

She'd scoured social media. It didn't appear that he had his own accounts, but she saw a handful of snapshots on Julien's pages. There'd been one at his friend Reece's wedding. Grant had been standing with the groom, Julien and Kennedy Aldrich.

There'd also been an older shot at Julien's birthday party, and the four friends were sporting neon-colored athletic shoes. None of the shots had been a close-up.

On the flight over, Aria had been nosy, asking Svetlana about Grant. The other woman had mysteriously said that he could be intense and liked to be in charge. Intrigued, Aria had pressed for more. Svetlana had said it would take a very special woman to be everything Grant needed. She'd hinted that the two of them had been a bit more than friends, but there had never been anything serious between them.

When Aria had pressed for more information, Svetlana had given one of her famous half-smiles and wished Aria luck finding out for herself. Purposefully, Svetlana had checked the altimeter then changed the subject to talk about her continuing trip to New York to meet with her future husband.

The conversation had left Aria frustrated. The more she'd tried to find out about Grant, the more he seemed like an enigma.

Nothing she'd seen or heard had prepared her for seeing him in person. A shiver ran through her. His features had an old-world ruggedness and his shoulders were impossibly wide. He was more masculine than she'd imagined, more commanding.

"Welcome to New Mexico." His voice was deep, friendly, reassuring, making her insides turn somersaults.

Her immediate, consuming attraction to him surprised her. "Grant Kingston, I presume?"

"At your service."

Even around successful, handsome men, Aria had always been completely confident. Until today. "I didn't expect you to come yourself."

"I'm the only Bonds employee in Los Alamos. You know Julien wouldn't have allowed me to send anyone else. And after everything Julien said about you, I was anxious to meet you. And I'm glad I came." He smiled.

The full power of its seducing effect smacked her. A feminine part of her melted in instinctive recognition. The sensation was as unusual as it was unwelcome.

"I've heard a few things about you, too." And it had made last night's sleep more than a little restless. If her guess was right, she wouldn't rest any easier tonight.

He extended his hand.

She slid her palm against his and found his hand big, his touch warm, reassuring. Nothing could have prepared her for the impact he'd had on her.

Grant held her hand a bit longer than socially acceptable. Maybe it was because of what Julien and Svetlana had said, but she was very much aware of Grant's strength and power. Aria's heart thudded, and she pulled back her palm so she wouldn't be tempted to stay forever.

He was smiling, but she thought there might be something slightly predatory beneath the welcome.

Aria lowered her sunglasses.

Since they stood so close, she noticed how deep and blue his eyes were, reminding her of an arctic lake. And damn, he smelled good. She inhaled the scent of his leather jacket, certainly, but there was more. Musk was layered in, along with the crisp rawness of the outdoors.

Mostly, he radiated power and confidence. To make things clear to both of them, she added, "Thanks for having me. I can't imagine you're happy about having an unwanted houseguest."

"Turns out I might not mind it as much as I thought I might."

Each word had been dragged across sandpaper. For a moment, just a wicked moment, she imagined him whispering her name as he unfastened her shirt.

Aria shook her head to clear it. No doubt she was attracted to him, and he'd made it clear it was mutual, but that didn't mean anything. She was a professional businesswoman, and she had never slept with anyone she'd worked with. She wouldn't allow Grant Kingston to be the first...

even if she had to constantly remind herself of that fact. "I'm good at taking care of myself, so you won't need to go out of your way to entertain me. I'll be a good houseguest."

"I'm sure you will."

An airport employee removed Aria's one big suitcase from the jet and hauled it toward the SUV.

"Can I help you with your briefcase or the other bag?" Grant asked.

"Actually, the duffel is for you."

"For me?"

"Svetlana asked me to give it to you. She said it's a gift from Julien."

"In that case, I'll definitely take it. God only knows what's in it."

"Oh? You've made me curious."

"I'll guarantee it would scare the boots right off your feet."

"Now I've got to see."

"No doubt whips, chains, handcuffs."

"You're not serious." She looked at him, unsure whether or not he was joking. And if he wasn't, what then? "Handcuffs?"

"Do you always rush into danger?"

Her pulse missed a beat. "Is that what I'm doing?"

"Yeah. Consider yourself warned."

Was that a statement or a dare? She shivered, and not from the cold, but rather from the anticipation his words sent through her.

Do you want to read more? Discover Command

ABOUT THE AUTHOR

I invite you to be the very first to know all the news by subscribing to my very special **VIP Reader newsletter**! You'll find exclusive excerpts, bonus reads, and insider information.

For tons of fun and to join with other awesome people like you, join my Facebook reader group: **Sierra's Super Stars**

And for a current booklist, please visit my **website**.

USA Today bestselling author Sierra Cartwright was born in England, and she spent her early childhood traipsing through castles and dreaming of happily-ever afters. She has two wonderful kids and four amazing grand-kitties. She now calls Galveston, Texas home and loves to connect with her readers. Please do drop her a note.

ALSO BY SIERRA CARTWRIGHT

Titans

Sexiest Billionaire

Billionaire's Matchmaker

Billionaire's Christmas

Determined Billionaire

Scandalous Billionaire

Ruthless Billionaire

Titans Quarter

His to Claim

His to Love

His to Cherish

Titans Quarter Holidays

His Christmas Gift

His Christmas Wish

Titans Sin City

Hard Hand

Slow Burn

All-In

Titans: Reserve

Tease Me

Titans Captivated

Theirs to Hold

Theirs to Love

Theirs to Wed

Hawkeye

Come to Me

Trust in Me

Meant For Me

Hold On To Me

Believe in Me

Hawkeye: Denver

Initiation

Determination

Temptation

Bonds

Crave

Claim

Command

Donovan Dynasty

Bind

Brand

Boss

Printed in Great Britain
by Amazon